STAR TREK™

OFFICIAL LICENSED PRODUCT

Gallery Books
A Division of Simon & Schuster, Inc.
1230 Avenue of the Americas
New York, NY 10020

First Gallery Books hardcover edition November 2012

GALLERY BOOKS and colophon are trademarks of Simon & Schuster, Inc.

For information about special discounts for bulk purchases, please contact Simon & Schuster Special Sales at 1-866-506-1949 or business@simonandschuster.com

The Simon & Schuster Speakers Bureau can bring authors to your live event. For more information or to book an event contact the Simon & Schuster Speakers Bureau at 1-866-248-3049 or visit our website at www.simonspeakers.com.

Designed by Lee Parsons
Edited by Derek Smith

Manufactured in the United States of America

10 9 8 7 6 5 4 3 2 1

ISBN 978-1-4516-9590-8
ISBN 978-1476-72568-0 (ebook)

KLINGON
BIRD-OF-PREY

I.K.S. ROTARRAN
(B'REL-CLASS)

OWNERS' WORKSHOP MANUAL

Rick Sternbach and **Ben Robinson**

CONTENTS

It was my choice to flag my Ninth Fleet as Supreme Commander with my beloved *Rotarran*. I had no use for the immensity, the sheer sluggishness, the inertia, the lack of acceleration and the unneeded armor of the giant battle cruiser of the *Vor'cha*-class, and especially I did not want to assume command aboard the *Negh'var*. That was Gowron's favorite fighting ship and may Kahless bless him and her for that marriage of personality and weaponry. But that is not my spirit. The *Negh'var* reflects nothing about me or my approach to battle. My approach to ship-to-ship confrontation is best embodied in the versatility, the speed, the incredible acceleration and appropriate weaponry found aboard the *Rotarran*, for any engagement from a known or unknown enemy.

For the known enemy, our weaponry is superior to any and all military craft in the four quadrants. For the unknown attacker, the *Rotarran*'s ability to instantly disappear into deep space to both the naked eye and all known and theoretical molecular scanning devices offers the most extraordinary strategic defense imaginable and has succeeded in saving my old skin on several occasions.

The *Vor'cha*-class may be capable of absorbing an attack by an entire fleet of warbirds and any known alien battle cruiser. My preference is to evade such an attack, not to absorb it, and return within nano-seconds from completely unexpected coordinates to neutralize the attack with minimal damage to my Flagship and the fleet. The *Vor'cha*-class cruiser is incapable of such tactics, thereby allowing massive collateral damage while awaiting cessation of the alien attack before turning to neutralize the enemy ship.

The only warship in the Klingon fleet capable of executing the swiftness and elusiveness of my preferred tactics in ship-to-ship warfare is the *B'rel*-class Bird-of-Prey. And of course, the precise specifications of the *Rotarran* are not known to anyone beyond myself and my most executive officers.

I am compelled to allow posterity and the military historians to evaluate the success and failure of my approach to close combat as opposed to that of Chancellor Gowron. Perhaps my tactics are rooted in my understanding of a young life lived on the streets of the Ketha Lowlands rather than in the more comfortable manor houses of the rich valleys surrounding the central plateau of the First City, the homeland of Chancellor Gowron.

As to which tactics are more effective, all I can offer is the hard truth that I am here, the House of Martok stands today, but the ruined House of Gowron is gone from the face of Qo'noS and gone from the annals of military victories of the Klingon Empire.

GENERAL MARTOK

SUPREME COMMANDER OF THE NINTH FLEET AND CHANCELLOR OF THE KLINGON EMPIRE

GENERAL MARTOK PORTRAYED BY J.G. HERTZLER

ᕟᒐᕑ ᕧᒐᑎ

The Bird-of-Prey is the classic Klingon starship. It is a fast and deadly scouting and raiding ship that has been at the heart of the Klingon Defense Force for centuries. The first examples even pre-date Klingon spaceflight. Small fighters with the same basic layout have been in use since early planetary conflicts. That design has been modified over the centuries, first to incorporate impulse engines, then warp engines. Even fundamental changes to the science have been incorporated into the same basic spaceframe. The Klingons have simply seen no need to change something that they believe is fundamentally correct.

By the late 2370s, the design of the Bird-of-Prey had been settled for over a century, but ships were produced at a variety of scales from vast *K'vort*-class battlecruisers to tiny scouting vessels. The archetypal version of the ship is the *B'rel*-class, a 139-meter long ship with seven decks and a crew of 36. The internal layout and even weaponry vary from ship to ship, but they are all capable of high warp speeds, and fitted with a cloaking device. To many Klingon minds it is the perfect fighting vessel—as fast, tough and deadly as its crew.

When the semi-mythical Klingon leader Kahless united the Klingon people over a thousand years ago, he established the great Klingon Military Academies, which are operated under the control of the High Council rather than by the individual Great Houses. The most famous of these are the Training Academy at Ogat and the Klingon Naval Academy on Dek'Go'Kor. The Klingon Naval Academy is responsible for the principal design and mass production of ships.

The Academy has far greater resources than even the most powerful of the Great Houses and has the remit of concentrating on large-scale technological developments in areas such as warp and impulse dynamics, and the fundamentals of spaceframe design. The Houses are then left to concentrate on the details of how the ships are fitted out and are much more likely to improve the design of weapons and shielding as they seek to find even the smallest advantage in combat.

Klingon design philosophy has always centered on tried-and-tested methods and places great importance on the ability to mass-produce ships at great speed. As such, it has concentrated on a handful of basic designs, which

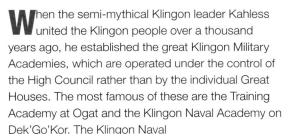

form the backbone of the Klingon fleet, the Bird-of-Prey and the battle cruiser being the most common. The modular design means that the maximum number of ships can be produced at the fastest possible rate.

Wherever possible, the same structural elements are scaled up or down to produce ships of different sizes. The Klingons are reluctant to make major structural changes to their starship designs, preferring to concentrate on improving the individual systems. As a result, Birds-of-Prey vary enormously in size from tiny *B'rel*-class scouting ships to vast *K'vort*-class cruisers. The larger of these ships are literally scaled up versions of the basic design even down to the size of the disruptor cannons, which

- **1** Defensive Shield Plating
- **2** Cloaking Field Emitter
- **3** Deck 4 Entry/Escape Hatch
- **4** Subspace Communications Antenna
- **5** Space Environment Sensor Group
- **6** Tactical Command Transceiver
- **7** Atmospheric Flight Flow Sensor
- **8** Deck 3 Cargo Bay External Access
- **9** Deck 3 Access Hatch
- **10** Deck 1 & 2 Dorsal Blister
- **11** Upper Wing Hinge Plates
- **12** Lower Wing Hinge Plates
- **13** Warp Field External Shaping Plates
- **14** Reaction Control System Thrusters
- **15** Warp Wing Induction Energy Storage
- **16** Warp System External Resupply Connections
- **17** Dorsal Aft Impulse Engines

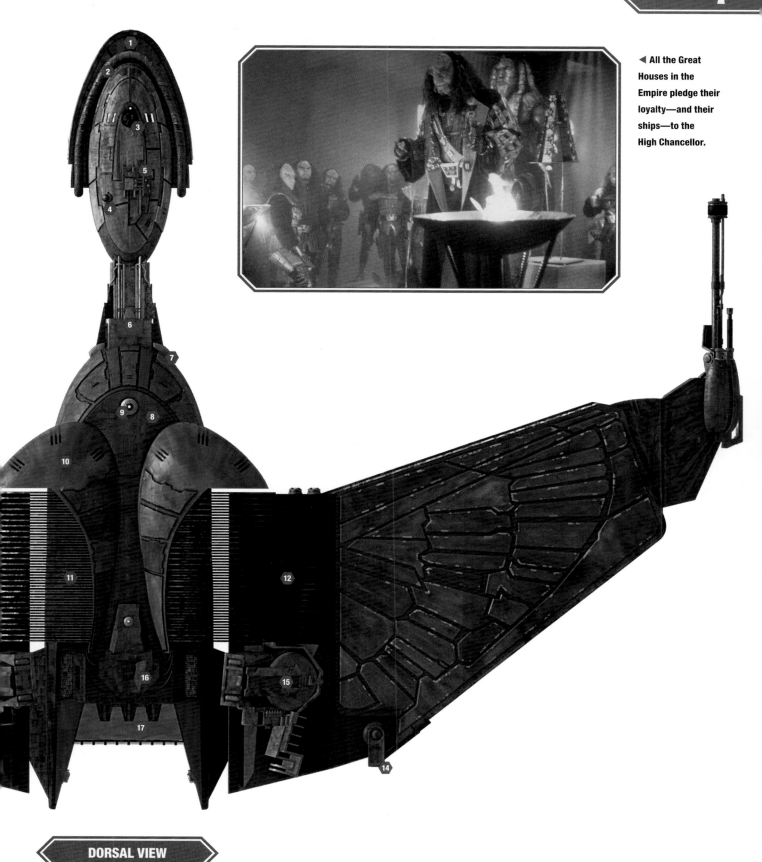

All the Great Houses in the Empire pledge their loyalty—and their ships—to the High Chancellor.

1. Central Navigational Deflector
2. Photon Torpedo Launcher
3. Emergency Subspace Buoys
4. Central Computer Core
5. Ventral Sensor Cap
6. Plasma Power Conduit
7. Forward Impulse Engine
8. Active/Passive Targeting Sensors
9. Port Warp Wing
10. Wingtip Disruptor
11. Secondary Disruptor Cannons
12. Primary Disruptor Cannon
13. Warp Field External Shaping Plates
14. Warp Wing Structural Reinforcements
15. Ventral Aft Impulse Engines
16. Deck 7 Loading Ramp
17. Tractor Beam Emitter

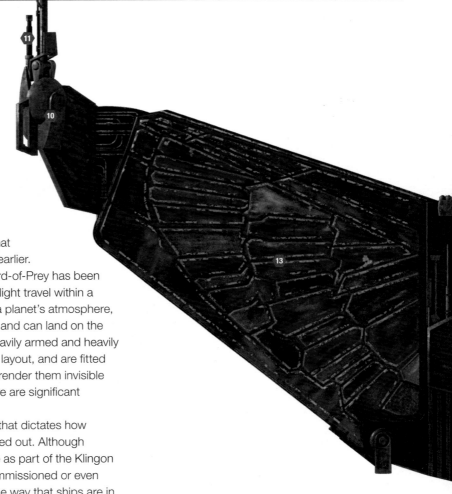

become enormous units that are almost as long as the smallest ships.

Of course, this approach means that Klingon ship design is rarely as innovative as that used by other groups such as the Federation and although there have been advances in warp and weapons technology, anyone looking at a Bird-of-Prey from the 2370s would instantly recognize it as being the same as models that were in use well over a century earlier.

For hundreds of years the Bird-of-Prey has been designed for warp flight, for sublight travel within a planetary system, and to enter a planet's atmosphere, where it is highly maneuverable and can land on the surface. All Birds-of-Prey are heavily armed and heavily armored, follow the same basic layout, and are fitted with a cloaking device that can render them invisible to sensors, but beyond this there are significant differences between each ship.

There is no central authority that dictates how a Klingon starship should be fitted out. Although almost all Klingon ships operate as part of the Klingon Defense Force, they are not commissioned or even operated by a central body in the way that ships are in the Federation or the Romulan Empire. Klingon society operates on feudal lines, with individuals and families pledging their allegiance to Houses, the greatest of which come together to form the Klingon High Council, which is led by the High Chancellor. It is these Houses

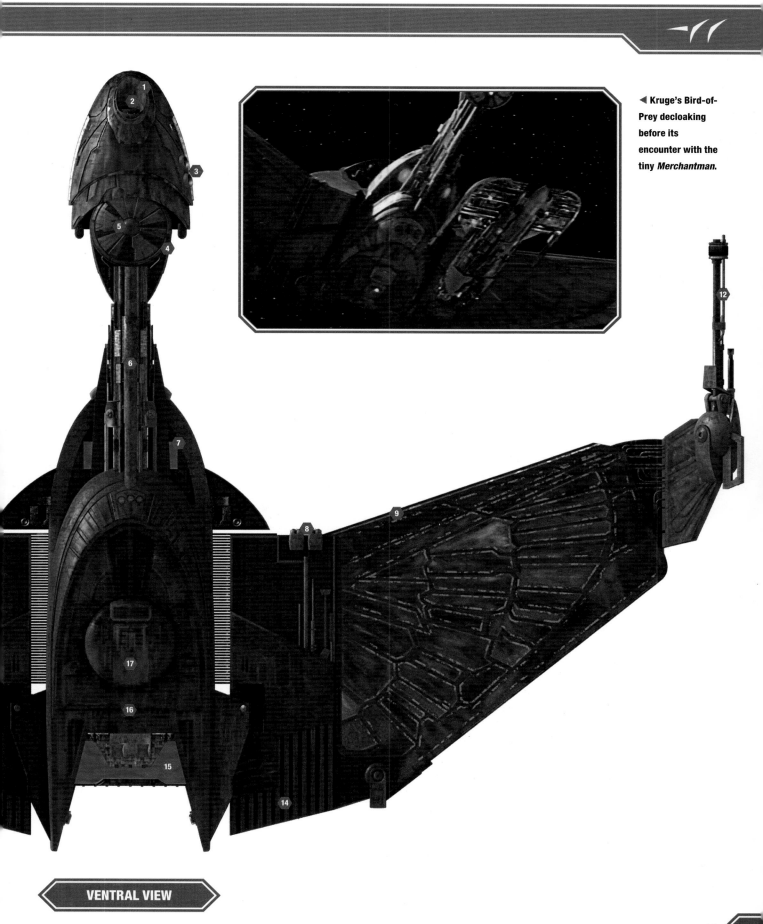

◄ Kruge's Bird-of-Prey decloaking before its encounter with the tiny *Merchantman*.

VENTRAL VIEW

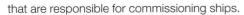

that are responsible for commissioning ships.

This means that individual Birds-of-Prey are fitted out very differently depending on the resources and personal preferences of the House that commissions them. One House may prefer speed and maneuverability over pure power; another may choose to fit its ships with phasers rather than disruptors. There are potentiality as many permutations as there are Klingon ships. It is a well-known saying that *no two weapons are the same*. This variety has proved a great strength in battle; for example, during the Dominion War one Klingon Bird-of-Prey, the *Ki'tang*, proved to be immune to the devastating Breen energy dampening weapon because it used a different tritium intermix to the other ships in the fleet.

Despite this enormous diversity in the way Klingon ships are equipped, the fundamental structure of the spaceframe is the same for almost every one and all Birds-of-Prey, whether they are raiders or cruisers, have the same basic layout with the bridge in the section at the head, above the photon torpedo launcher, and the impulse and warp engineering sections at the rear between the wings, which generate the warp fields. The disruptor cannons are always at the tips of the wings, and the bottom of the ship always features a landing ramp that can be extended to the ground.

When a House is ready to commission a ship, it contacts the Naval Academy shipyards and arranges payment. The shipyards then assign a *renwI'*, or architect, to the project and he meets with the

1. Defensive Shield Plating
2. Central Navigational Deflector
3. Photon Torpedo Launcher
4. Cloaking Field Emitter
5. Subspace Communications Antenna
6. Active/Passive Targeting Sensors
7. Warp Wing
8. Reaction Control System Thrusters
9. Deck 1 & 2 Dorsal Blister
10. Lower Wing Hinge Plates
11. Short Range Sensors
12. Disruptor Cannon Structural Extension
13. Wingtip Disruptor
14. Secondary Disruptor Cannons
15. Primary Disruptor Cannon
16. Upper Wing Hinge Plates
17. Warp Wing Induction Energy Storage
18. Warp Wing Structural Reinforcements
19. Dorsal Aft Impulse Engines
20. Ventral Aft Impulse Engines
21. Deck 7 Loading Ramp

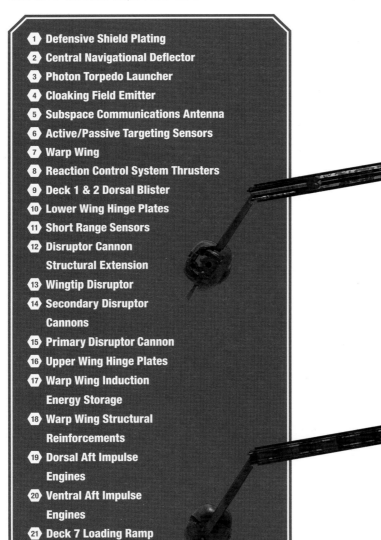

▲ The Bird-of-Prey is one of the most common ships in the Klingon fleet and is the ideal scouting and raiding vessel.

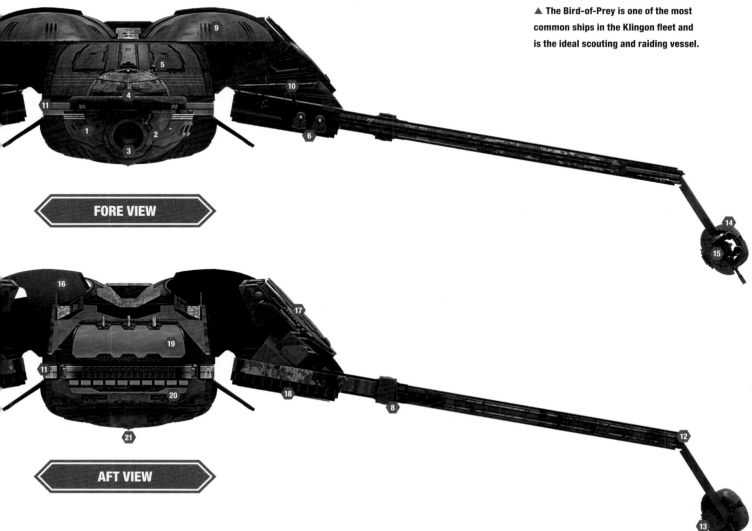

FORE VIEW

AFT VIEW

STARBOARD VIEW

1. Cloaking Field Emitter
2. Central Navigational Deflector
3. Defensive Shield Plating
4. Space Environment Sensor Group
5. Ventral Sensor Cap
6. Central Computer Core
7. Plasma Power Conduit
8. Atmospheric Flight Flow Sensor
9. Short Range Sensors
10. Lower Wing Hinge Plates
11. Upper Wing Hinge Plates
12. Warp Wing Induction Energy Storage
13. Reaction Control System Thrusters
14. Warp Field External Shaping Plates
15. Disruptor Cannon Structural Extension
16. Wingtip Disruptor
17. Secondary Disruptor Cannons
18. Primary Disruptor Cannon

representatives of the House to discuss the exact fit and specifications of the ship. The standard Bird-of-Prey is the 139-meter *B'rel*-class scout. This is the starting point for every version of the ship and is by far the most common. When a Bird-of-Prey is scaled up, the basic vehicle spaceframe remains proportionally the same, with extra decks being added as the ship increases in size.

However, most Klingon commanders are happy with the standard sized ship. The disagreements tend to come when the shipyard has to fit the engines and weapon systems. Not all Klingons appreciate the compromises that are needed to produce an effective ship and there are stories of Klingon Houses insisting on overpowered engines and dangerously over-specced disruptors. The *renwI'* has a duty to reign in these excesses and to produce a good fighting ship. It is not unheard of for these disagreements to end in violence and accordingly the architects are among the most physically impressive and skilled non-warriors in the Klingon Empire. It is a position of great honor since it is one of the rare roles that allows a common civilian to tell a noble warrior that he is wrong.

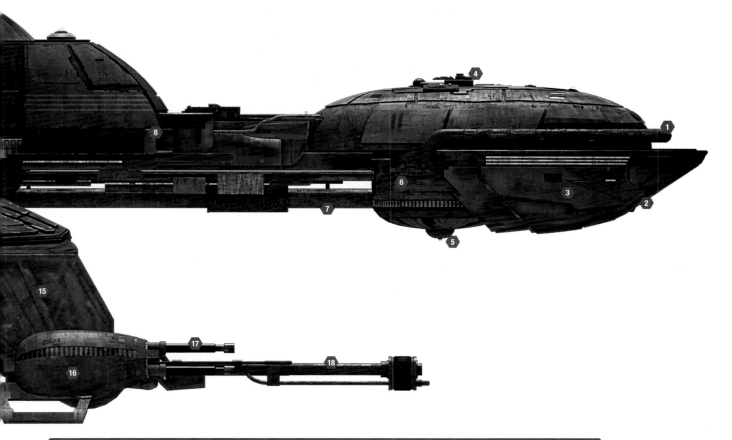

◄ Klingon Birds-of-Prey fought on both sides of the Klingon civil war that followed K'mpec's death and captains such as Kurn became important men.

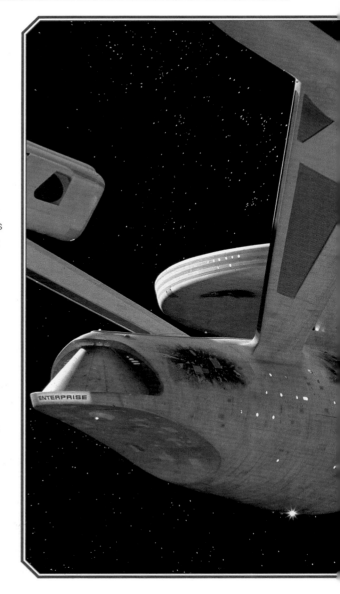

◥ **The internal layout of a Bird-of-Prey can vary enormously from ship to ship. Commander Kruge favoured an unusual design of bridge that put him on a raised platform.**

The wiser houses understand exactly what it takes to make a good fighting ship, which, according to the Klingon bards, should be like a finely balanced blade, quick to respond to the hand but heavy and sharp enough to cut deep. As a result there is such a thing as a classic Bird-of-Prey and any differences normally relate to the internal layout, the kind of torpedoes carried and the precise balance between maneuverability and power.

One of the defining characteristics of the Bird-of-Prey's design is the Klingons' devotion to multiple redundancies. All the ship's important systems operate in pairs—or multiples—of interconnected systems. Thus there are twin warp cores, and 12 impulse engines that produce forward propulsion (a further pair of impulse engines produces downward 'thrust'). Even the EPS (electroplasma) conduits that distribute power around the ship operate in branching pairs.

If one of the systems is completely knocked out there is another to take over its duties, but this isn't simply a case of one system coming into play when another fails; the systems on a Bird-of-Prey are interconnected and permanently operating. This means that if one of the warp cores isn't functioning at full capacity, the other one can take on a portion of its load to compensate. The Klingons have taken the system even further so the impulse and warp engines are tied into one another and can supplement each other if one of them is severely damaged.

By designing their ships this way, the Klingons are following the nature of their own bodies, which have a similar form of redundancy known as *brak'lul*. For example, the Klingon body has 23 ribs (double the number found on a human being), two livers, and an

eight-chambered rather than four-chambered heart.

In many ways this system of multiple redundancies could be seen as wasteful. In some cases it means forcing barely compatible systems to work together in ways that other cultures wouldn't even attempt, but it also makes Klingon ships remarkably tough and as a consequence they can withstand more damage than almost any comparable vessel.

The biggest differences between individual Birds-of-Prey are often seen in the internal layout. The interior bulkheads are designed to be repositionable, so that a commander can choose how the internal volume is divided. A *B'rel*-class ship is actually surprisingly spacious for the standard crew of 36, but in some cases commanders still insist on making their

crews share quarters and devoting disproportionately large areas to cargo. Even after the ship has been commissioned the bulkheads can be moved around easily, converting a raiding ship into a troop transporter that is suitable for delivering warriors to the front line of a ground-based battle.

Whereas the outside of a Bird-of-Prey rarely varies, the design of the bridges can be as different as the men who command them. Some versions are dominated by throne-like command chairs on raised platforms with the other bridge officers seated in a well around the edge of the room; others use a periscope-like device that descends from the deck above and allows the commander to target the weapons personally. The most common version places the

▼ **Kruge's Bird-of-Prey confronts the *Constitution*-class *U.S.S. Enterprise* in orbit around the Genesis planet.**

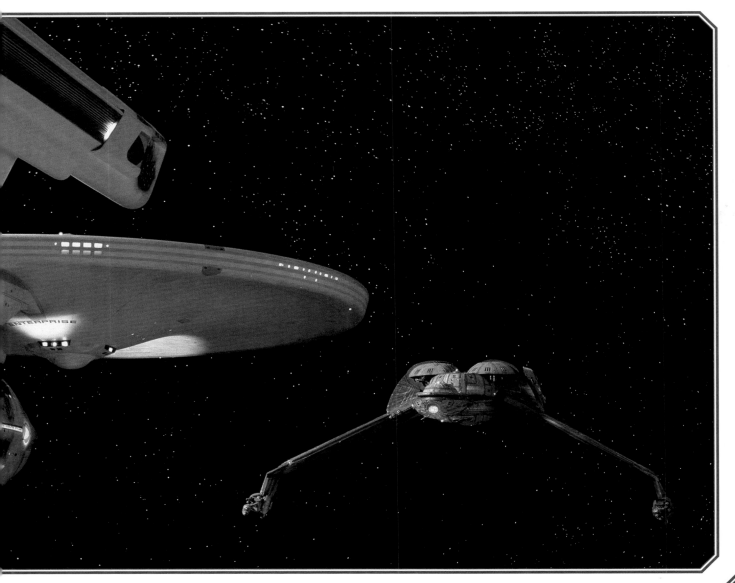

◥ Some Birds-of-Prey have featured a periscope-iike device that the captain uses to target the weapons.

commander in the center of the room, with the helm and navigation stations directly in front of him, his first officer behind him and other bridge stations around the perimeter of the room.

Once a Bird-of-Prey is completed it is delivered to the House that commissioned it, and under Klingon tradition, instantly pledged to serve in the Klingon Defense Force. Klingon Houses vary enormously in size. The most powerful Houses consist of thousands of men, and may control hundreds of ships. For example, in the early 23rd century the House of Jarod controlled over 250 ships. At the opposite end of the scale a smaller House might control just a single ship.

Following Kahless's reforms, the Houses all agreed to send their men and ships to serve in the Klingon Defense Force. The administration of this is controlled by the High Council and the major appointments are

made by the High Chancellor himself. In theory, the Houses only hold their possessions with the consent of the High Chancellor, who can revoke their privileges and take control of their ships and lands. However, the Chancellor is rarely in a position to do this, and depends on the support of the more powerful houses. As a result, senior appointments can depend as much on family connections as on personal excellence.

In the centuries after Kahless, the Great Houses all pledged their allegiance to an Emperor, but in practice individual captains and the leaders of the Houses formed an often uneasy alliance that kept the Empire together. Little has changed in the last thousand years and as such the captain of a Klingon ship has very real political power.

The leader of a Great House appoints the captain and crew of each ship, and their first loyalty is almost always to him before the Emperor or the High Chancellor. In times of conflict it is not uncommon for the Houses to form power blocks that are opposed to the High Chancellor or one another. It is less common, but not unheard of, for the captains of individual ships to disobey orders given by the leader of their House and choose their own side in a conflict.

The individual Houses also have their own facilities for developing new weapons, and as soon as cloaking technology was acquired several of the more powerful Houses started looking for ways to overcome its limitations. Scientists from the House of Chang managed to develop the device to a point where ships could actually fire while cloaked. Because of the way Klingon society operates, this technology was not shared with the other Houses or the Klingon Defense Force. Chang preferred to keep the technology to himself and to use it in a bid for power.

▶ In the 2290s General Chang used a prototype Bird-of-Prey with an advanced cloaking device to disrupt peace negotiations with the Federation.

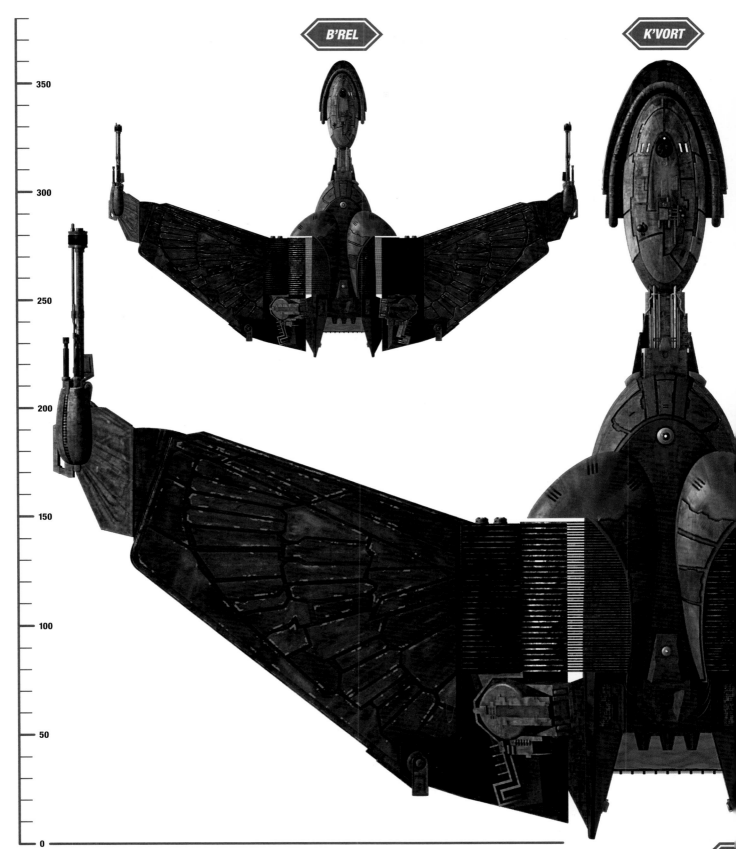

350

300

250

200

150

100

50

0

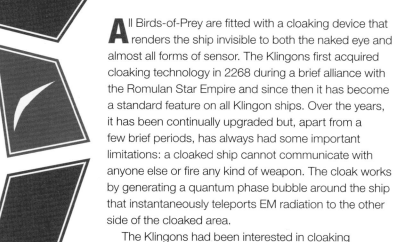
All Birds-of-Prey are fitted with a cloaking device that renders the ship invisible to both the naked eye and almost all forms of sensor. The Klingons first acquired cloaking technology in 2268 during a brief alliance with the Romulan Star Empire and since then it has become a standard feature on all Klingon ships. Over the years, it has been continually upgraded but, apart from a few brief periods, has always had some important limitations: a cloaked ship cannot communicate with anyone else or fire any kind of weapon. The cloak works by generating a quantum phase bubble around the ship that instantaneously teleports EM radiation to the other side of the cloaked area.

The Klingons had been interested in cloaking technology since their first encounters with the Romulans in the 22nd century, but Klingon scientists had never been able to develop an effective version of their own. By the mid-2260s both the Klingon and Romulan empires had become concerned about the expansion of the United Federation of Planets, which was growing at the fastest rate in its history. The Federation, which had been at war with both empires, was gaining new members and resources at a phenomenal rate. Although the Romulans and Klingons were extremely suspicious of one another it was clear to them that they were in danger of being marginalized.

The Romulans had emerged from isolation in 2266 and tried the Federation's defenses with a new generation of cloaked ship. Although the cloaking technology appeared promising, the ship failed to return, leading many in the Romulan military to feel that it was underpowered. In particular they were concerned that Federation ships had greater firepower, better defenses and could achieve higher speeds.

The following year the Klingons launched an all-out war against the Federation, but were halted by an extremely powerful species, called the Organians, who imposed a peace treaty on them. To many Klingons the Organian peace treaty seemed to favor the Federation, since it set up a system where the control of unaligned worlds was determined by the economic rather than military benefits either power could offer. The Klingons were concerned that the Federation was acquiring valuable resources that would leave them much better equipped for war.

In late 2267, a Romulan delegation approached the Klingon Empire, offering them access to cloaking and computer technology in return for starship designs and disruptor technology. Many members of the Klingon High Council were suspicious of the Romulans' motives, but the lure of cloaking technology proved too great and by early 2268 the Romulan Senate and the Klingon High Council had signed a treaty that provided for a limited exchange of technology and offered guarantees about encroaching into one another's space.

The first *D7*-class Klingon cruisers were delivered to the Romulans within a matter of months, while the Romulans handed over four working cloaking devices. The cloaking devices required a certain amount of modification before they could work with the Klingon ships—in particular the Klingon warp engines had to be realigned to reduce their radiation emissions, and top speeds had to be cut to avoid detection. The cloaking devices also required constant monitoring. Only a handful of engineers in the Imperial Fleet understood how to operate them and Klingon captains had little idea of how to adjust their tactics.

The Federation was so alarmed by this development that they risked a major diplomatic incident by breaching the Romulan Neutral Zone and stealing a cloaking device from one of the newly supplied *D7* battle cruisers. The Klingons proved that Starfleet's concern was justified the following year, when the Klingon commanders Kor and Kang took two cloaked divisions of *D5* battle cruisers to launch a surprise attack on Caleb IV. The attack was devastating and became known as a famous victory.

However, even at this early stage the Romulan-Klingon alliance was showing signs of stress. Despite the assurances given in the treaty, the Romulans took advantage of their new battle cruiser technology to annex several disputed worlds along the Klingon-Romulan border. The Klingons retaliated and within a matter of months the treaty was in tatters.

▶ The Klingons first acquired cloaking technology in 2268 as part of a technology exchange with the Romulans. In return the Romulans gained access to the designs for Klingon battle cruisers.

◄ The cloaking
device normally
prevents a cloaked
ship from firing
its weapons. This
limitation was
briefly overcome by
General Chang in
the early 2290s who
developed a Bird-
of-Prey that could
fire torpedoes while
cloaked.

Meanwhile, the Federation appeared to be developing new countermeasures against the cloaking device. The balance of power had shifted, and although hostilities continued, the Klingons drew back from all-out war. They took advantage of the situation to roll out the technology to the entire Imperial Fleet, in a massive program that saw every ship from the tiniest scout to the largest warship fitted with a cloaking device.

The Great Houses set their scientists to improving the cloak and overcoming its limitations, which prevented a cloaked ship from firing any kind of weaponry. By 2292 the House of Chang had developed a prototype Bird-of-Prey that could fire while cloaked. This relied on a special modification that allowed photon torpedoes to be fired through the cloaking field. Since the prototype was destroyed and Chang did not make the technology available to the Klingon Defense Force, it is not absolutely clear how the modification worked. It is thought to have involved an active, energized surface material that was built into the torpedo housings. This meant that the torpedoes could pass through the cloaking field without being affected by the spatial distortion. The modifications reduced the overall effectiveness of the cloak, and exposed the General's vessel to repeated—and fatal—return fire from Starfleet's *Enterprise* and *Excelsior* starships.

After the 2270s the Klingons and Romulans did not share cloaking technology until the Dominion War and as a result the approaches have diverged slightly. The Romulans in particular have experimented with methods of moving an entire ship out of phase with the normal universe, not only making it undetectable but potentially immune to weapons fire. The Klingons have concentrated on methods of firing while cloaked. To date neither of these approaches have met with lasting success.

The Dominion War posed such a great threat that the Klingons and the Romulans eventually allowed a modification of their treaties with the Federation so that the *U.S.S. Defiant* could be equipped with a cloaking device. Klingon scientists had to redouble their efforts to improve the cloaking device after it emerged that the Dominion could detect cloaked ships. The cloak remains a vital asset for the Klingon Empire, despite its controversial history connected with the Romulans, and it is now impossible to imagine a Bird-of-Prey that cannot conceal itself from its enemies.

▼ During the
Dominion War the
Klingon Empire
modified its treaties
with the Federation
to allow the
Federation to equip
one of its warships,
the *U.S.S. Defiant*,
with a Romulan
cloaking device.

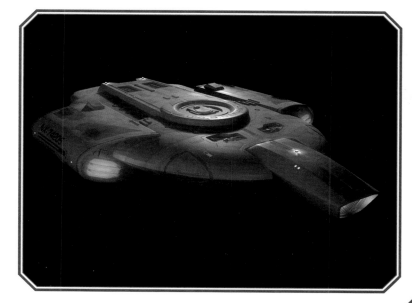

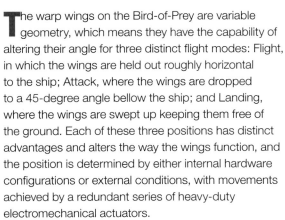

The warp wings on the Bird-of-Prey are variable geometry, which means they have the capability of altering their angle for three distinct flight modes: Flight, in which the wings are held out roughly horizontal to the ship; Attack, where the wings are dropped to a 45-degree angle bellow the ship; and Landing, where the wings are swept up keeping them free of the ground. Each of these three positions has distinct advantages and alters the way the wings function, and the position is determined by either internal hardware configurations or external conditions, with movements achieved by a redundant series of heavy-duty electromechanical actuators.

The wings are each attached to the hull structure by way of a substantial hinge assembly 1.74 meters in diameter outboard of Deck 5. Six identical pairs of rotational mounts are gamma welded to each side of the aft hull and to each wing box in a microgravity assembly fixture. The fixture is equipped with 235 precision optical and magnetic sensor guides to align the hinge sections to accept the tempered duranium center cylinder.

Six pairs of actuator motors and multiple position and torsion sensors are integrated within the rotational joints. When the wings are moved, the actuators are controlled by the central computer according to the ship's real-time flight mode, or commanded by the helm officer within the flight safety limits perceived by the navigational system. Normal motion rates are kept to within 5–8 degrees per second while in space, though emergency motor power can be applied to move though 14 degrees per second. Power for the actuators comes from three pairs of medium step-down plasma nodes.

In the flight position the wings take on the role that is served by warp nacelles on most other vessels, with superheated plasma energizing warp coils to create a warp field around the ship. When the Bird-of-Prey is in this mode the wings are generally level with the horizontal plane of the ship and with each other. Standard warp flight for the Bird-of-Prey involves energy fields that move the vessel most efficiently when they are coplanar, emanating from the warp plates vertically and aft and interacting only minimally above or below the ship.

The transverse plasma conduit connecting the warp reactors to the wings on Deck 5 incorporates a rotating joint, which is fully open in the cruise configuration. This allows for the most speed and faster-than-light (FTL) maneuvering options in transport or battle situations.

Attack maneuvers with the disruptors powered up require the wings to transition to the dropped position, at least 43 degrees away from horizontal. This transition can occur while the ship is slowing from warp to sublight, and in fact the lowered wings can facilitate the bleed-off of warp field energy. This procedure is sometimes used as a braking tactic to allow a Bird-of-Prey to switch from being pursued to becoming the pursuer. The dropped wings create a constriction in the warp plasma conduit necessary for the disruptors to pressurize properly and form plasma bolts dense enough to inflict major damage.

Disruptor bolts can be fired at more flattened angles, though the energy contained in each bolt will be diminished. In some cases, this may be enough to disable an enemy vessel, especially if boarding and not

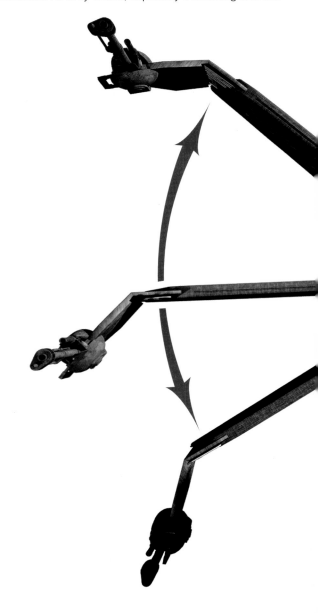

immediate destruction is the objective. The attack position has the added benefit of protecting the lower decks in the aft hull, where the warp cores are situated, plus the ship's neck structure from certain angles. While the defensive shield grid and armor plating remain the primary lines of defense, the wings can shadow the ship from incoming energy weapons fire or projectile weapon detonation.

Landing position elevates the wings to approximately 40 degrees above the plane of the hinge. This procedure lifts the wingtip disruptors safely above ground level and minimizes hardware impacts with support crews and maintenance equipment. It also helps to center the wing mass over the deployed landing gear. The wingtip separation

distance is decreased, allowing for touchdowns in areas that might be slightly less open than at dedicated bases. Once on the ground, the wings can be lowered for repair work or routine checks.

Structural rigidity at each flight position is enhanced by two distinctive sets of interleaved hinge plates on each side of the ship. The upper halves are attached to the hull, the lower halves to the warp wing box. The plates, fabricated from duranium titanide, are allowed to slide past each other until exposed to a modified tractor field, which causes them to grab and lock. The locked plates are particularly helpful during planetary landings and takeoffs where the wings need to be supported against gravity, even with the help of the mass-lightening impulse engines.

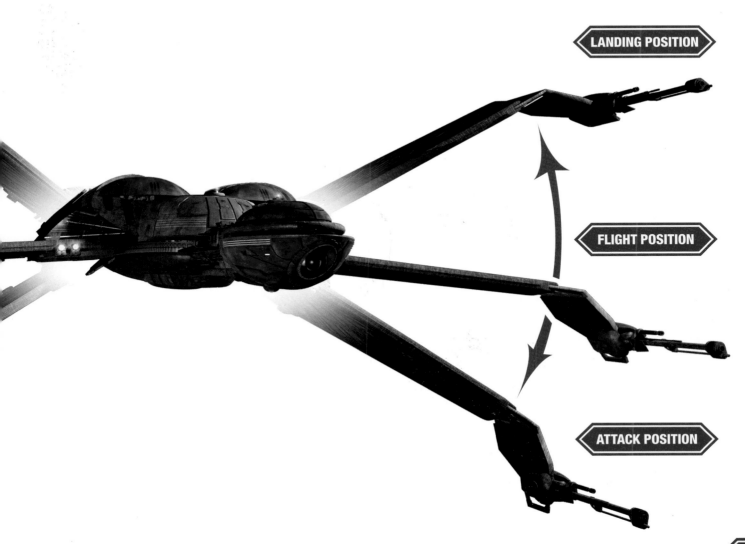

LANDING POSITION

FLIGHT POSITION

ATTACK POSITION

I.K.S. ROTARRAN

ROTARRAN

The *I.K.S. Rotarran* is a typical *B'rel*-class vessel, designed for swift raids and brutal combat. Under General Martok, who made her his flagship, she played a vital role in the Dominion War, when she took part in many famous conflicts including the Battles of Chin'toka and Cardassia. Her victories under Martok's command made her one of the most famous ships in Klingon history.

In terms of layout there was nothing extraordinary about the *Rotarran*—she had standard weaponry and engines, with wingtip plasma disruptors and the classic twin warp cores. If anything she was even leaner than other Birds-of-Prey, with Martok placing great store in the traditional Klingon virtues of spartan living and devotion to duty.

Since the end of the Dominion War and Martok's elevation to High Chancellor, the *Rotarran* has been held up as something of an ideal as if she were the perfect Bird-of-Prey and she is the subject of several operas and epic poems. The reality is much more complicated. For example, the crew was not exclusively Klingon and even Martok himself freely admits that the *Rotarran* wasn't always well maintained, that the warriors aboard were a ragbag bunch of veterans and raw recruits and they often owed their survival as much to luck as skill. But all of this adds to the legend and few Klingon warriors believe there could have been anything more glorious than serving on the *Rotarran* as she plunged into the heart of the Dominion fleet.

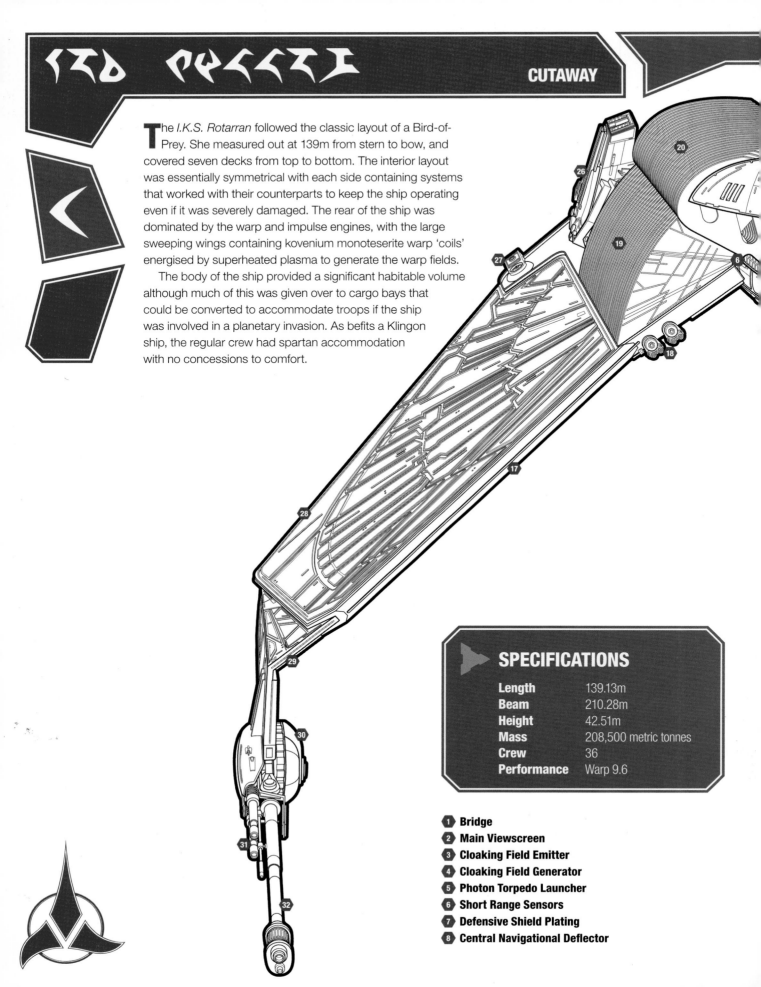

The *I.K.S. Rotarran* followed the classic layout of a Bird-of-Prey. She measured out at 139m from stern to bow, and covered seven decks from top to bottom. The interior layout was essentially symmetrical with each side containing systems that worked with their counterparts to keep the ship operating even if it was severely damaged. The rear of the ship was dominated by the warp and impulse engines, with the large sweeping wings containing kovenium monoteserite warp 'coils' energised by superheated plasma to generate the warp fields.

The body of the ship provided a significant habitable volume although much of this was given over to cargo bays that could be converted to accommodate troops if the ship was involved in a planetary invasion. As befits a Klingon ship, the regular crew had spartan accommodation with no concessions to comfort.

SPECIFICATIONS

Length	139.13m
Beam	210.28m
Height	42.51m
Mass	208,500 metric tonnes
Crew	36
Performance	Warp 9.6

1. **Bridge**
2. **Main Viewscreen**
3. **Cloaking Field Emitter**
4. **Cloaking Field Generator**
5. **Photon Torpedo Launcher**
6. **Short Range Sensors**
7. **Defensive Shield Plating**
8. **Central Navigational Deflector**

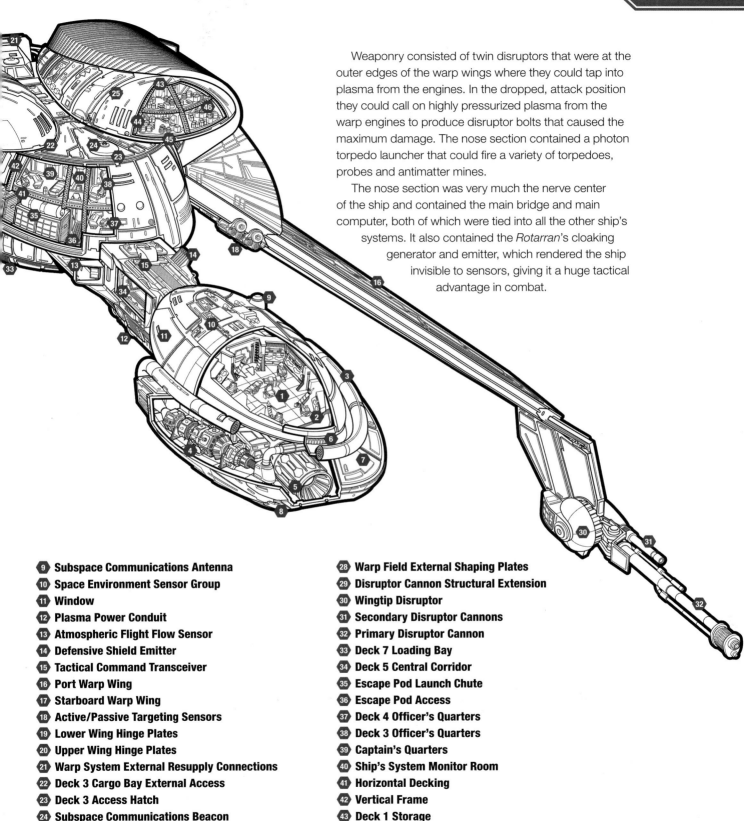

Weaponry consisted of twin disruptors that were at the outer edges of the warp wings where they could tap into plasma from the engines. In the dropped, attack position they could call on highly pressurized plasma from the warp engines to produce disruptor bolts that caused the maximum damage. The nose section contained a photon torpedo launcher that could fire a variety of torpedoes, probes and antimatter mines.

The nose section was very much the nerve center of the ship and contained the main bridge and main computer, both of which were tied into all the other ship's systems. It also contained the *Rotarran*'s cloaking generator and emitter, which rendered the ship invisible to sensors, giving it a huge tactical advantage in combat.

9 **Subspace Communications Antenna**
10 **Space Environment Sensor Group**
11 **Window**
12 **Plasma Power Conduit**
13 **Atmospheric Flight Flow Sensor**
14 **Defensive Shield Emitter**
15 **Tactical Command Transceiver**
16 **Port Warp Wing**
17 **Starboard Warp Wing**
18 **Active/Passive Targeting Sensors**
19 **Lower Wing Hinge Plates**
20 **Upper Wing Hinge Plates**
21 **Warp System External Resupply Connections**
22 **Deck 3 Cargo Bay External Access**
23 **Deck 3 Access Hatch**
24 **Subspace Communications Beacon**
25 **Deck 1 & 2 Dorsal Blister**
26 **Warp Wing Induction Energy Storage**
27 **Reaction Control System Thrusters**

28 **Warp Field External Shaping Plates**
29 **Disruptor Cannon Structural Extension**
30 **Wingtip Disruptor**
31 **Secondary Disruptor Cannons**
32 **Primary Disruptor Cannon**
33 **Deck 7 Loading Bay**
34 **Deck 5 Central Corridor**
35 **Escape Pod Launch Chute**
36 **Escape Pod Access**
37 **Deck 4 Officer's Quarters**
38 **Deck 3 Officer's Quarters**
39 **Captain's Quarters**
40 **Ship's System Monitor Room**
41 **Horizontal Decking**
42 **Vertical Frame**
43 **Deck 1 Storage**
44 **Deck 2 Storage**
45 **Bloodwine Barrel**
46 **General Storage Container**

There was little indication that the *Rotarran* would become so famous when she was built at Dek'Go'Kor in 2358 by the House of Gowron. At the time Gowron was building a political power base outside the High Council and the *Rotarran* was one of several ships under his control that patrolled the outer reaches of Klingon space.

After K'mpec died in 2367 the *Rotarran* was recalled to the heart of the Klingon Empire and took part in the Klingon Civil War, but although she was involved in a handful of skirmishes with ships loyal to the House of Duras, she wasn't engaged in any major conflicts. Following Gowron's victory, the *Rotarran* was assigned to patrol the Klingon-Cardassian border and consequently was part of the fleet that massed at

Deep Space Nine in 2371 when Gowron declared war on Cardassia.

The *Rotarran* spent the next year fighting Cardassians with some success and the crew distinguished themselves with several notable victories, but when the Dominion entered the war things changed dramatically. The crew were horrified to discover that their ship was outgunned by the Jem'Hadar, who were routinely overpowering Klingon ships. For seven months, the *Rotarran* did little but run from her enemies. The crew became increasingly demoralised and dissatisfied. By mid-2372, they were convinced that victory was impossible, and that they were never destined to reach the gates of the Klingon Valhalla, *Sto'vokor*.

▶ The ***Rotarran*** was commanded by General, later Chancelllor, Martok. Under his command she became famous as the ideal Klingon fighting ship.

However, at this point Gowron put General Martok in charge of the *Rotarran* and she began what would become a famous career. She earned a stunning series of victories in the Dominion War that culminated in her leading the Klingon fleet in the Battle of Cardassia.

Martok's period in command did not begin well. He had only recently been rescued from a Dominion prison camp and his spirit was nearly broken. The crew he inherited were in an even worse state—constant defeats had broken their morale and left them in despair.

During the first mission Martok avoided combat and his very un-Klingon caution did nothing for the crew's spirits. His lack of confidence actually led to him being challenged by his first officer, Worf. However, winning that challenge helped to rekindle his warrior spirit and the *Rotarran* completed her first mission by destroying a Jem'Hadar fighter and rescuing 35 Klingon survivors from the battle cruiser *B'Moth*.

The months that followed were bloody ones for the *Rotarran*, but under Martok's command she became an efficient and deadly fighting ship. When the Dominion took control of *Deep Space Nine* she joined the combined Starfleet and Klingon forces based at Starbase 375, with the Second Fleet. This phase of the war was especially hard, with the Klingon and Federation forces constantly being forced back, but the *Rotarran* was revitalized under her new commander and scored some significant victories that culminated in the her leading the Klingon forces that helped to retake *Deep Space Nine* in the first significant Alliance victory of the war.

Shortly afterward, Martok was made commander of the Ninth Fleet. Rather than move his flag to a larger, more prestigious battle cruiser, he chose to keep it on the *Rotarran*, believing that a Bird-of-Prey was a true fighting ship and emphasising that he would lead from the front rather than from a flagship far behind the lines.

The next months saw Martok record some famous victories aboard the *Rotarran*, including one of the most important Alliance victories of the war – the Battle of Chin'toka, where the *Rotarran* distinguished herself. In early 2375, the *Rotarran* mounted the famous raid that saw her ignite a solar flare that destroyed the Monac shipyards.

Of course, the Dominion War was far from an endless succession of victories, and the *Rotarran* was one of only 14 Alliance ships to survive the disastrous Second Battle of Chin'toka, where the Breen Confederacy joined the Dominion and used a previously unknown form of energy dampening weapon to inflict a devastating defeat on the Alliance forces. Weeks later she barely survived the misguided attack on Avenal VII.

However, the *Rotarran* not only survived but was upgraded to resist the Breen weapons and was in the vanguard of the Alliance fleet that took Cardassia, finally bringing an end to the Dominion War in 2375. Martok himself had become Klingon High Chancellor in the weeks preceding the battle, but insisted on keeping his trusted Bird-of-Prey as his flagship, and as a result the *Rotarran* ended the Dominion War almost as famous as her illustrious commander and her deeds are still celebrated in songs throughout the Klingon Empire.

▼ Martok regained his warrior's spirit, when Worf made him fight for command of the *Rotarran*.

◄ The *I.K.S. Rotarran* fires on a Jem'Hadar attack ship during the Dominion War.

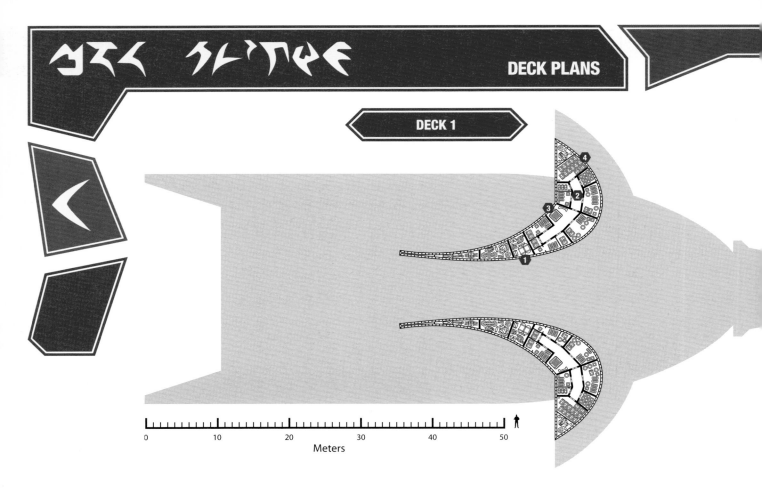

DECK 1

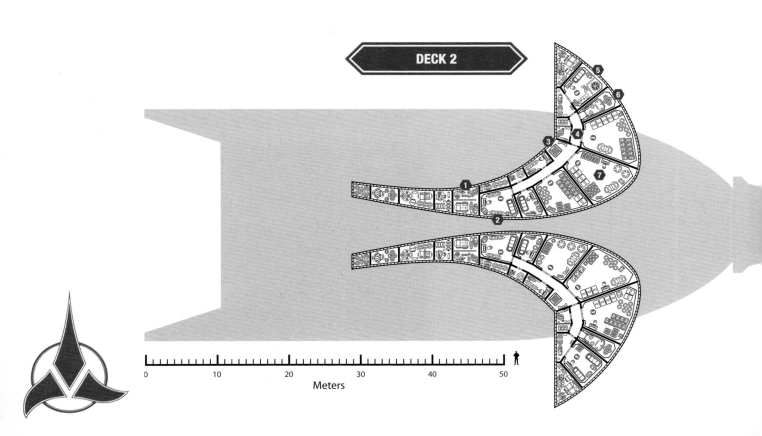

DECK 2

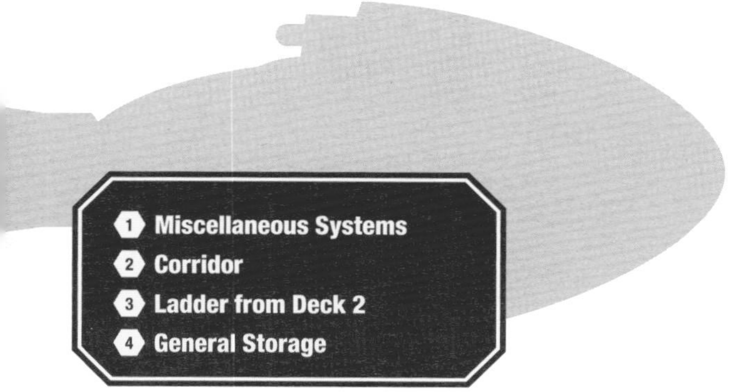

1 Miscellaneous Systems
2 Corridor
3 Ladder from Deck 2
4 General Storage

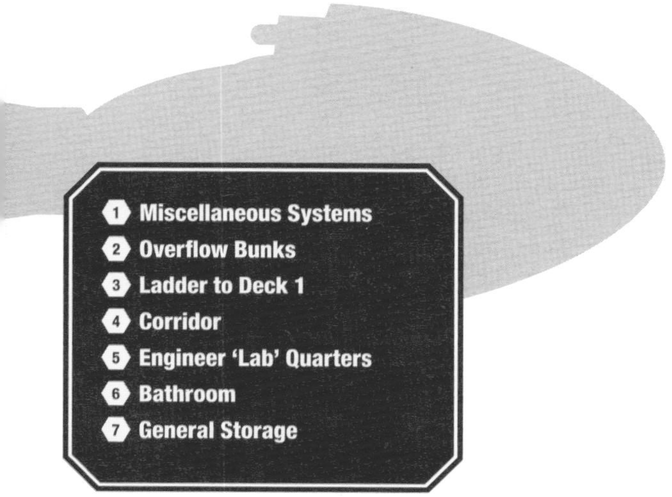

1 Miscellaneous Systems
2 Overflow Bunks
3 Ladder to Deck 1
4 Corridor
5 Engineer 'Lab' Quarters
6 Bathroom
7 General Storage

KEY TO HARDWARE

POWER GROUP

 EPS SWITCHING NODE

 POWER FREQUENCY INVERTER

 BACKUP POWER CELLS

 PRIMARY CAPACITOR BANK

 KLYSTRON RELAY

 STRUCTURAL INTEGRITY FIELD GENERATOR

 INERTIAL DAMPING FIELD GENERATOR

 ELECTROHYDRAULIC SYSTEMS

COMMAND AND CONTROL GROUP

 SMALL MONITORING CONSOLE

 MULTI-OPERATOR CONSOLE

 SYSTEMS CONTROL STATION

 SYSTEMS DISPLAY REPEATER

 DEDICATED HARDWARE ACTIVATION

 COM PANEL

FABRICATION SUBSYSTEMS

 MOLDS & COATINGS SUBSYSTEM

 SIX AXIS MATERIAL SHAPER

 MATTER SEPARATOR

TRANSPORTER SYSTEMS

 EMERGENCY TRANSPORTER

 GENERAL PERSONNEL TRANSPORTER

WARRIOR/CARGO TRANSPORTER

SENSOR AND COMMUNICATIONS GROUP

○ INTERNAL SENSOR

SENSOR DATA PREPROCESSOR

INTERNAL COMMUNICATIONS NODE

EXTERNAL RF COMMUNICATIONS ANTENNA

EXTERNAL SUBSPACE ANTENNA

SUBSPACE RADIO ASSEMBLY

EMERGENCY BEACON

ATMOSPHERE HANDLING GROUP

 ATMOSPHERE RECIRCULATOR

 LOCAL CONTAMINANT SCRUBBER

 LARGE ATMOSPHERIC SCRUBBER

 DUAL-GAS LIQUIFIED ATMOSPHERIC STORAGE

EMERGENCY OXYGEN SUPPLY

SPACECRAFT HARDWARE ELEMENTS

 LADDER

 REPAIR BENCH

 SUB-FLOOR ACCESS

 SMALL CARGO CONTAINERS

 MEDIUM CARGO CONTAINERS

 COLD STORAGE CARGO

VACUUM OR PRESSURIZED CARGO

BLOODWINE BARRELS

FLUID HANDLING GROUP

 RESERVE DEUTERIUM FUEL STORAGE

IMPULSE DEUTERIUM FLOW CONTROLLER

 DEUTERIUM CHILLER ASSEMBLY

 TYPE I FLUID STORAGE

TYPE II FLUID STORAGE

TYPE III FLUID STORAGE

 WATER-ONLY STORAGE

 COOLANT RECIRCULATION

 WASTE FLUIDS PROCESSING

CONDUIT PURGE FLUID RESERVOIR

SODIUM HEAT EXCHANGER

PRESSURIZATION GAS SPHERE

 FLUID SCRUBBER/SEPARATOR

 STANDARD FLUID PUMP

CRYOGENIC RECIRCULATOR

DECK 3

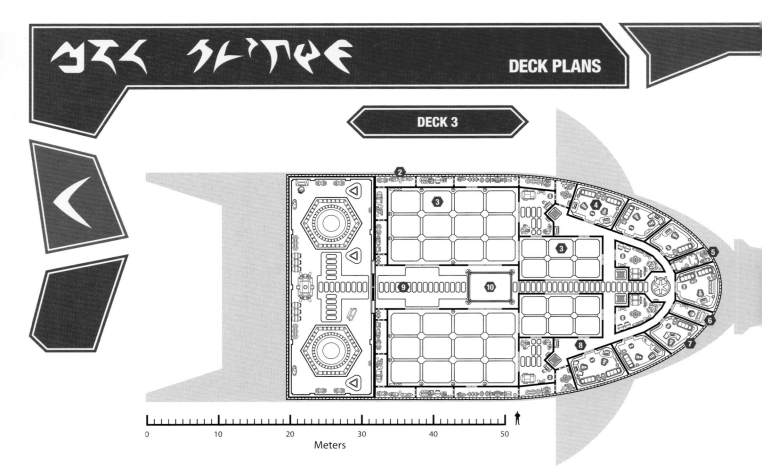

DECK 4

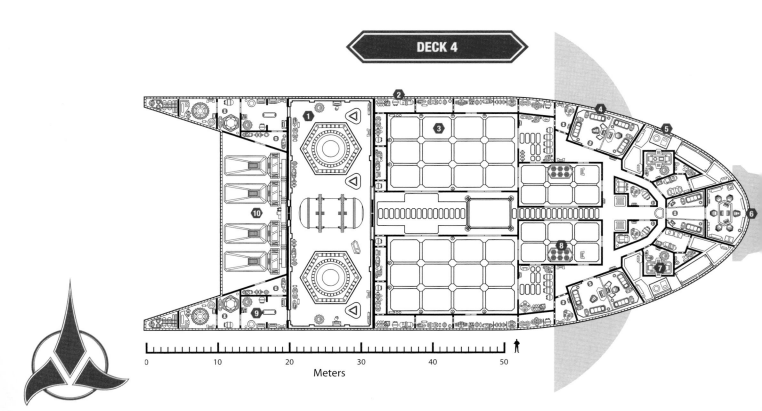

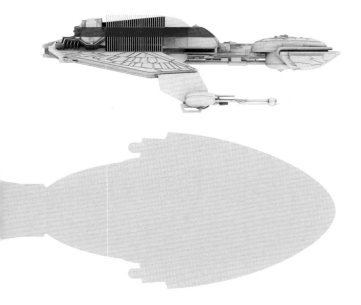

1. Main Engineering
2. Miscellaneous Systems
3. Cargo Bay
4. Quarters
5. Bathroom
6. Computer Systems
7. Captain's Quarters
8. Corridor
9. Transfer Aisle
10. Elevator

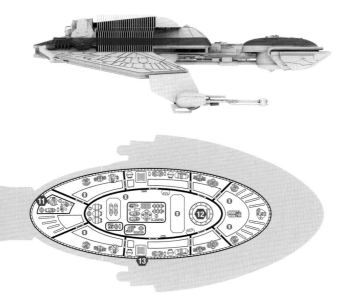

1. Main Engineering
2. Miscellaneous Systems
3. Cargo Bay
4. Quarters
5. Escape Pod Chutes
6. Tactical Conference Room
7. Forward Impulse Engine
8. Transporter Pad
9. Engineering Support
10. Upper Impulse Engines
11. Sensor and Communication Systems
12. Ladder to Deck 4 Entry/Escape Hatch
13. Ladder from Deck 5

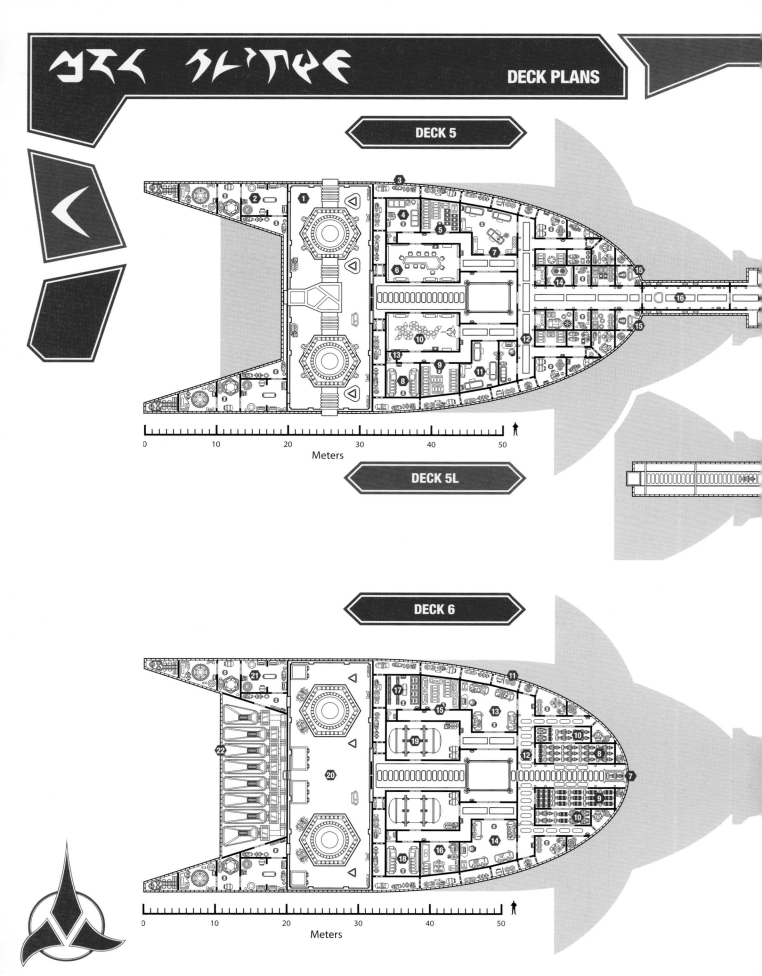

DECK 5

DECK 5L

DECK 6

Meters

Meters

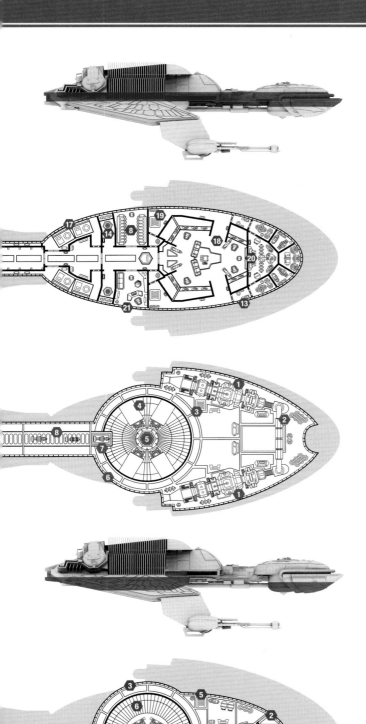

1 Main Engineering	**12** Transverse Corridor
2 Impulse Engineering Support	**13** Bathroom
	14 Transporter Room
3 Systems	**15** Auxiliary Control
4 Food Preparation	**16** Central Corridor
5 Consumables Storage	**17** Escape Pod Chutes
6 Mess Hall	**18** Bridge
7 Medical Bay	**19** Ladder to Deck 4
8 Weapons Lockers	**20** Sensor & Communciations Systems
9 Warrior Gear Storage	
10 Training Hall	
11 Medical Bay Overflow	**21** Ready Room

1 Cloaking Generator	**5** Computer Core Access Well
2 Generator Transverse Plasma Conduit	
	6 Catwalk
3 Ladder to Decks 5 & 6	**7** Cargo/Torpedo Elevator
4 Computer Core Processor Module	**8** Cargo/Torpedo Transfer Track

1 Torpedo Launcher	**13** Port Fabrication & Repair
2 Docking Vestibule	
3 Catwalk	**14** Starboard Fabrication & Repair
4 Cargo/Torpedo Transfer Track	
	15 Raw Materials Storage
5 Ladder from Deck 5L	
6 Lower Computer Core	**16** Molding & Coating Facility
7 Cargo/Torpedo Elevator	
	17 Astronics Repair & Storage
8 Port Torpedo Storage	
9 Starboard Torpedo Storage	**18** Weapons Lockers
	19 Deuterium Fuel Storage
10 Torpedo Special Ops	
11 MIscellaneous Systems	**20** Main Engineering
	21 Engineering Support
12 Transverse Cargo/ Torpedo Track	**22** Lower Impulse Engines

With few exceptions, every mission of a *B'rel*-class Bird-of-Prey will involve the use of at least one active weapon in the ship's arsenal as well as the defensive shields, subspace signal intelligence devices, and stealth measures such as the cloaking generator.

The two primary weapon systems chosen by every modern Klingon commander are the plasma-powered disruptor cannon and the photon torpedo. Variants of both weapons have been available throughout the history of the vessel class and have been honed to a high degree of efficiency and lethality, often with an 'acceptable' trade-off of higher risk to the safety of the crews using them. Disruptors run hot from increased plasma pressures and shot frequency, and photon torpedoes have been known to detonate prematurely or track friendly targets, but the Empire continues to produce large quantities of weapons that it knows are proven in battle.

Protecting a Bird-of-Prey goes hand in hand with its offensive systems. High-energy EM shield envelopes stop most beam weapons and torpedoes early in a fight, backed up by hardened hull plating and structural integrity fields. False identifier codes, deceptive sensor echoes, and communications meant to confuse the enemy are all tools accessible to the warrior crews. Energy for all main systems, including weapons and defense, comes from the ship's twin warp cores, which are doubly surrounded by additional layers of plating. Perhaps the most intriguing use of that power lies in the cloaking generator, which renders the ship nearly invisible in all wavelengths to an adversary's sensors. While the majority of the *B'rel*-class vessels cannot fire weapons when cloaked, the Galaxy was witness to a Bird-of-Prey that could, and future developments from the Empire must be closely watched...

The Bird-of-Prey's primary weapons are twin disruptor cannons at the tips of the wings. In contrast to Federation ships, which use phasers—a form of directed energy beam—the disruptor cannons fire bolts of superheated plasma that is drawn from the warp engines, through the wings and into the cannon itself, where it is compressed and accelerated before it is fired.

Each disruptor assembly consists of primary and secondary cannons, two stages of accelerator, superconducting toroids that hold a reserve supply of plasma, a cryogenic system that cools the disruptor after it is fired, targeting systems and torsion arms that can adjust the exact angle of fire, and krogium particle injectors, which bind the plasma together so that it doesn't dissipate before it is delivered to its target.

The cannons are most effective when the wings are in the down position. In this alignment, internal systems constrict the central conduit putting the plasma under greater pressure and increasing the energy density, all of which makes the plasma bolt more powerful. Plasma bolts can, of course, still be fired with the wings in the horizontal and even in the landing position, but the plasma has a far lower energy yield and causes less

▼ **The Bird-of-Prey's twin disruptor cannons fire compressed bolts or streams of plasma that are drawn from its engines.**

damage. For this reason, a Klingon commander will typically lower the wings to the 'attack' position before dropping the cloak.

Today's standard Bird-of-Prey wing-mounted disruptor weapon retains a number of operational features originally developed in the 2140s, most importantly those related to the way the components connect with one another.

Superhot plasma generated by the twin warp cores is channeled into the wingtip disruptor assemblies for compression, acceleration, and firing. Redundant conduits off the main wing plasma tunnel converge on the disruptor plasma supply duct, and from there feed into the first-stage accelerator and superconducting reserve toroids.

The first-stage accelerator uses power generated by the warp cores to spin up and compress discrete streams of plasma that can take two possible routes. One is to proceed to the second-stage accelerator that feeds the main cannon, and the other is to be discharged through two secondary cannons.

The maximum energy released by the secondary cannons is typically 12.43 megawatts, and the plasma bolts can be shaped into pulses of variable lengths with variable delays between them. Low-power mode on the secondary cannons, involving energies down to a few hundred kilowatts, can be utilized for non-destructive marking and heating tasks.

Plasma sent to the second-stage accelerator is further compressed to a density of nearly 1500 kilograms per cubic meter and tightly wound up in a spiral magnetic field to a diameter of 1.57cm. The temperature at the center of the stream is some 120,000K (215,000°F), though the length of time the weapon is exposed to such extreme temperatures is measured in milliseconds and the disruptor cryo cooling system draws away the waste heat.

The second stage also employs a controlled injection of krogium excelinide particles, which are inherently unstable and must be kept in magnetic suspension. As they decay into their constituent quarks, these particles form seed points for the higher energy plasma to bond to temporarily while in flight from the main cannon, keeping the bolt in a tight package. The energy release in a main cannon pulse can reach 35.78 megawatts.

The main cannon is connected to the second-stage accelerator by a computer-controlled EM gate valve. The valve is constructed from a single block of forced-matrix duranium tritonide and carbon nano-

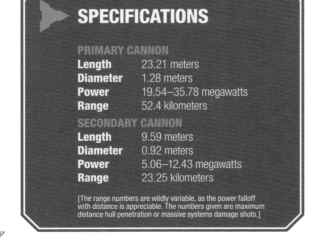

SPECIFICATIONS

PRIMARY CANNON

Length	23.21 meters
Diameter	1.28 meters
Power	19.54–35.78 megawatts
Range	52.4 kilometers

SECONDARY CANNON

Length	9.59 meters
Diameter	0.92 meters
Power	5.06–12.43 megawatts
Range	23.25 kilometers

[The range numbers are wildly variable, as the power falloff with distance is appreciable. The numbers given are maximum distance hull penetration or massive systems damage shots.]

whiskers. The dual-pulse irises are machined from disks of the same material. The firing commands to actually open and close the irises come from local weapon subprocessors within the wing structure, which monitor the plasma conditions in the system. The subprocessors operate on a set of stored instructions from the main computer dealing with target type, range, and velocity. Once the firing command is issued from the bridge, the subprocessors automatically configure the plasma bolts.

Targeting is accomplished through the processing of data collected by on-board short-range sensors located all around the ship, local attitude and velocity data from internal sensors, and specific narrow-angle boresight data read by the disruptor system. Computed firing solutions are handed off to the disruptor, integrated with the stored subprocessor codes, and adjustments are made to the cannon aiming system if necessary. This aiming system consists of electromotive servos connected by torsion and compression/extension arms to the main cannon. The cannon can be pitched or yawed within a 1.5-degree wide circle in 0.01 seconds, and multiple shots can be adjusted during firing.

In the event of power fluctuations from the main warp cores during combat situations, the disruptor system contains two superconducting reserve toroids that hold

1. **First-stage Accelerator**
2. **Combiner Gate Valves**
3. **Secondary Disruptor Cannons**
4. **Plasma Supply Duct**
5. **Second-stage Accelerator**
6. **Disruptor Cannon**
7. **Low-pressure Vent Tube**
8. **Targeting Boresight System**
9. **Torsion Arms (pitch axis)**
10. **Compression/Extension Arm (yaw axis)**
11. **Superconducting Reserve Torus 1**
12. **Superconducting Reserve Torus 2**
13. **Krogium Injector Assembly**
14. **Krogium Suspension Supply Tank**
15. **Magnetic Release Coil**
16. **Main Emitter**
17. **Narrow Angle EM Sensor**

densified plasma at high sublight speeds, available to make up for most power losses. The toroids are replenished at the first available moment after a shot volley.

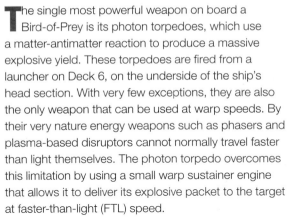

The single most powerful weapon on board a Bird-of-Prey is its photon torpedoes, which use a matter-antimatter reaction to produce a massive explosive yield. These torpedoes are fired from a launcher on Deck 6, on the underside of the ship's head section. With very few exceptions, they are also the only weapon that can be used at warp speeds. By their very nature energy weapons such as phasers and plasma-based disruptors cannot normally travel faster than light themselves. The photon torpedo overcomes this limitation by using a small warp sustainer engine that allows it to deliver its explosive packet to the target at faster-than-light (FTL) speed.

The torpedo launcher is structurally connected to the floor of Deck 6, and to the underside of Deck 5L above. It is designed to fit an ellipsoidal hole in the outer pressure hull that is 8.33 meters long by 5.56 meters wide. The launcher itself is based on a reinforced shell of duranium titanide that is 9.79 meters long and 3.87 meters in diameter. The interior of the aft pressure chamber is lined with gamma welded tungsten krellide to assist in heat rejection and to cradle the torpedo in an annular force field before firing.

It is powered by capacitor banks on Deck 6, with recharging accomplished through the ship's main plasma conduits. The conduits also provide an initial gas pressure boost to the torpedo. Data connections through both decks lead aft to the central

▼ **The photon torpedo launcher is fitted to the head of the Bird-of-Prey on Deck 6.**

computer core and up to the tactical station on the bridge as well as other key locations throughout the ship for remote firing.

Torpedoes, mines, and probes are normally stored in the aft hull on Deck 6. They are brought up to the level of Deck 5L, just below the main corridor, and travel forward along a maglev-equipped passageway similar to a Starfleet Jefferies tube. The projectiles are dropped back to the Deck 6 floor to the torpedo loader by articulated antigravs. The loader can accommodate torpedoes up to 1.13 meters in diameter and 3.01 meters long. The loader alcove envelopes the torpedo in a lift field and pushes it into the pressure chamber, where the breech door rotates and seals the system for firing.

During combat, a least four torpedoes are in the launcher processing area at any time and can comprise a mixed loadout. Volleys or single shots will trigger additional torpedoes to be sent forward from protected racks. A warrior designated as weapons loadmaster ensures that the weapon selection and transfer operations go smoothly.

Preliminary targeting data is handed off to the torpedo through either RF or subspace radio links throughout the loading process and updates can continue being transmitted after firing. With the breech door closed and a force field in place across the tube opening, the firing signal triggers three main actions in the launcher. A timed burst of plasma through magnetic gate

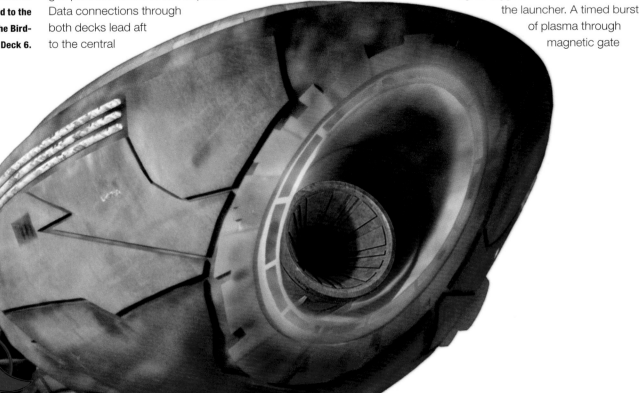

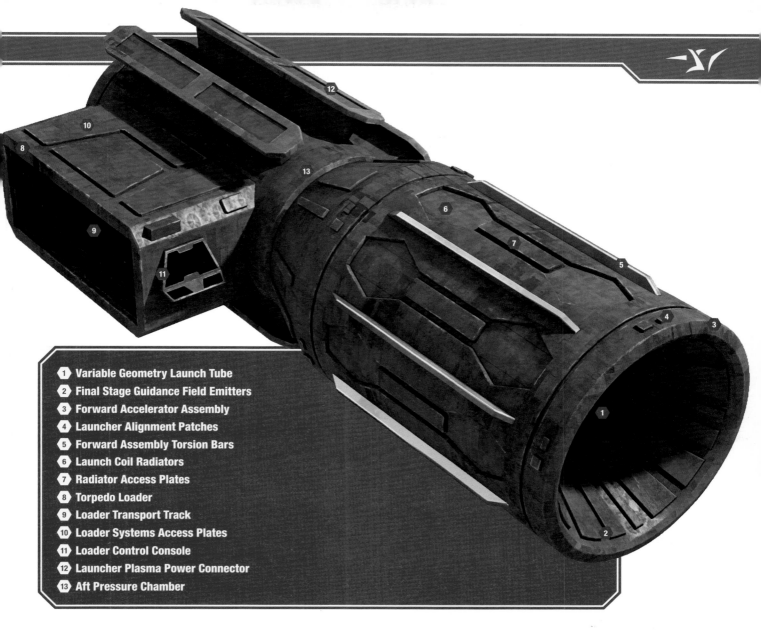

1. Variable Geometry Launch Tube
2. Final Stage Guidance Field Emitters
3. Forward Accelerator Assembly
4. Launcher Alignment Patches
5. Forward Assembly Torsion Bars
6. Launch Coil Radiators
7. Radiator Access Plates
8. Torpedo Loader
9. Loader Transport Track
10. Loader Systems Access Plates
11. Loader Control Console
12. Launcher Plasma Power Connector
13. Aft Pressure Chamber

valves pressurizes the aft chamber in approximately 0.013 seconds. The torpedo is kicked at roughly 600 meters per second into the mass driver coils, which at maximum power deliver an additional 12,400 meters per second velocity, ship relative. Simultaneously, the tube cover force field collapses and the weapon is away.

Once a torpedo has been fired its own on-board warp engine provides its velocity, but when it is fired, the launcher uses a forward accelerator assembly comprising six mass driver coils, which fire in sequence to launch the torpedo at high speed.

The launcher system can be configured for a wide range of initial firing velocities, depending on whether the weapon is being fired at sublight or at warp. High initial velocities are usually reserved for unpowered projectiles fired at warp, to afford the Bird-of-Prey maximum opportunity to bank away before the projectile's speed decays to sublight.

High launch velocities for powered torpedoes can also inflict greater damage at either impulse or warp. Slower launch velocities are common for stealthy missions, including the deployment of antimatter mines or more conventional explosive packages, and intelligence-gathering probes.

If the torpedo is launched at warp speed, the final small on-board engines are used to maintain FTL velocity and for terminal weapon guidance. Waste energy generated by the system is pumped through the forward opening by a set of radiators surrounding the accelerator.

Certain scout versions of the B'rel-class are not equipped with a torpedo launcher but are instead outfitted with a tight-beam long-range sensor dish. The disruptor cannons remain unchanged, however.

Between the outer shell of the torpedo launcher and the inner edge of the pressure hull are narrow hatchways and force field emitters that allow for crew passage during docked operations.

The current standard photon torpedo carried on the Bird-of-Prey is known as the Talon's Strike or *pach peng*, and is the most highly produced Klingon ordnance at 230,000 units per year. Each round measures 0.67 meters in diameter and 2.23 meters in length and masses 315.42 kilograms fully loaded.

The warp sustainer propulsion section and warhead casing are unremarkable duranium and tritanium alloys, while the forward guidance seeker and shield penetrator head is fabricated from layered tungsten, kratysite, and beryllium blesanide, similar to the alloys used in the ship's self-destruct charges.

The warp sustainer consists of three deuterium tanks, each feeding two microfusion engines, which are gimbaled to provide everything from minor terminal guidance steering to active target-chase maneuvers.

The warhead consists of a spherical lattice of highly magnetic borotenite alloy, into which antideuterium is injected and held in suspension. Unlike Starfleet torpedoes, which react deuterium and antideuterium in a central chamber, the Talon's Strike antimatter charge reacts directly with its higher density borotenite container.

The sensors in the forward penetrator are designed to seek out defensive shield subspace emissions, plus passive and active hull scan echoes. Detonation hardware is not usually required, as the weapon impact is generally enough to fracture the warhead and eliminate the antimatter containment. However, a small programmable explosive delay charge is included for special conditions, such as particularly tough enemy shields.

PHOTON TORPEDO: TALON'S STRIKE

1. **Enemy Shield Subspace Emission Detector**
2. **Active/Passive Forward Guidance Sensors**
3. **Lateral Gudiance Sensors**
4. **Forward Guidance Assembly**
5. **Structural Integrity Reinforcement**
6. **Warhead Access Plate**
7. **Warhead Assembly**
8. **Launch Energy Field Guide Bars**
9. **Propulsion Section Data Channels**
10. **Deuterium Fuel Tank (3)**
11. **Microfusion Engine Cowling**
12. **Microfusion Engine Nozzle (6)**

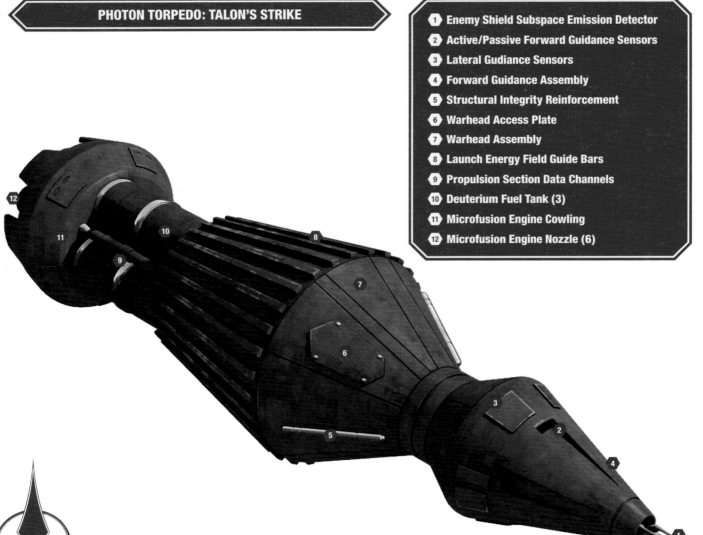

The second torpedo type, Morath's Fist or *moratlh ro'* is the most recent design, and was introduced in the 2360s. It was originally designed to be deployed aboard the *Vor'cha*-class attack cruisers, but has been sized to fit the *B'rel*-class.

The casing was originally conceived as a one-man escape pod, the baseline hull was adapted for torpedo use to hold a large magnetic torus of borotenite and antimatter plus twin deuterium-fueled warp sustainer engines.

The casing is 0.69 meters across at the widest point, 1.32 meters long, 0.59 meters tall, and masses 238.45 kilograms. A stretched variant to accommodate a larger torus has been built at 2.13 meters.

While the shell of the torpedo is very different to the standard Talon's Strike, most of the internal components are similar, owing to standardized fabrication techniques that have served the Empire well. The system was designed to create the maximum explosive charge and as a result the torpedo is overloaded with antimatter and the magnetic field generators are underpowered. This means that it is not considered safe after six months and must be either fired or refurbished.

This torpedo design has also been adapted for most of the stealth probe missions, when the warhead is replaced with a suite of intelligence sensors for both autonomous and real-time remotely piloted flights. The probe versions are equipped with shield generators plus self-destruct packages in the event of possible capture.

PHOTON TORPEDO: MORATH'S FIST

1. **Planar Sensor Array**
2. **Forward Short Range Sensors**
3. **Proximity Sensors**
4. **Upper Long Range Seeker**
5. **Shield Bubble Generator**
6. ***Vor'cha* Torpedo Hull**
7. **Warp Sustainer Engines**

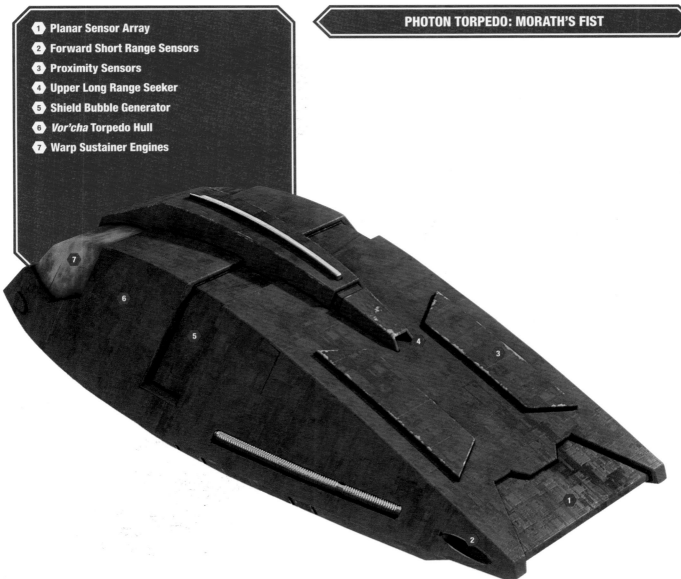

In addition to the standard designs of photon torpedo the Bird-of-Prey carries a kind of ordinance that can be deployed as both a photon torpedo and an antimatter mine distribution system.

This torpedo type, known as the Eagle's Claw is assembled from two antimatter mines and a shortened version of the Talon's Strike propulsion unit. A third mine can be added if time permits before engaging an enemy. The maximum diameter is 0.52 meters and the length with two mines is 1.56 meters, with a total mass of 253.65 kilograms.

The Eagle's Claw [*notqa' pach*] can be deployed in a wider array of tactical missions than the standard Talon's Strike. The torpedo can be fired as a standard offensive round, but can also be released at low velocity to separate into its component parts.

In standard torpedo mode, the entire unit is fired and operates in exactly the same way as the Talon's Strike, although the shortened engine section reduces its effective range. When the antimatter mines are deployed the combined unit is fired from the torpedo launcher at low velocity and the warp sustainer engine takes the torpedo to a pre-programmed location. The complete assembly then lies in wait using short-range scanners to search for an enemy vessel. When a target vessel is detected, the engine fires up again and propels the Eagle's Claw toward it. On-board proximity detectors then alert the torpedo to separate and the components then impact at multiple points on the target causing maximum damage. The Eagle's

ANTIMATTER MINE: EAGLE'S CLAW

1. **Guidance Seeker Head**
2. **Forward Proximity Sensors**
3. **Stealth Data Antenna**
4. **Lateral Proximity Sensor**
5. **Shield Bubble Generator**
6. **Antimatter Mine Assembly**
7. **Deuterium Fuel Tank (3)**
8. **Terminal Guidance Thrusters**
9. **Microfusion Engine Cowling**
10. **Microfusion Engine Nozzle (6)**

Claw can be programmed to activate at a variety of ranges. The shorter the distance between activation and impact, the better, since as soon as the engine is activated it will be detected by an approaching vessel, which given sufficient time can respond by raising its shields, significantly reducing the damage inflicted by the mine.

Torpedoes kept intact with their propulsion units can lie dormant for an indefinite period of time, ready to reignite their engines and head for targets of opportunity.

Each antimatter mine contains a borotenite lattice, programmable detonator, and proximity sensors, but also a low-power shield generator built into the outer casing. While not a full cloak, the shield diffuses enemy scans just enough to confuse their readings, making it extremely difficult to detect the mines.

Individual mines can be sent towards known in-space or planetside locations. As with the Talon's Strike, the Eagle's Claw is equipped with a target discriminator to separate friendly forces from enemy,

but inevitably history is rife with examples of this circuit being bypassed during Klingon factional conflict.

One standard tactic calls for the Eagle's Claw to be fired from the launcher at warp speed, and then to position itself behind the ship in order to target a pursuing vessel. However, this has serious limitations since the targeting sensors have to make incredibly fast calculations to place the mine in the path of a vessel traveling at faster-than-light speed. It has also been noted that most ships brave enough to pursue a Klingon Bird-of-Prey have their shields raised, limiting the amount of damage that would be inflicted by the mine.

The Eagle's Claw can also be used to deploy antimatter mines in a more conventional minefield. In this case, a large number of Eagle's Claw torpedoes are launched and onboard engines take them to predetermined positions a suitable distance from one another. The unit then separates into its component parts and the engine unit flies away from the minefield, removing a significant number of energy signatures that could be used to detect the minefield.

▲ Antimatter mines can be fired like photon torpedoes and then dispersed to create a minefield.

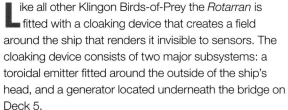

Like all other Klingon Birds-of-Prey the *Rotarran* is fitted with a cloaking device that creates a field around the ship that renders it invisible to sensors. The cloaking device consists of two major subsystems: a toroidal emitter fitted around the outside of the ship's head, and a generator located underneath the bridge on Deck 5.

This cloaking field acts to mask the presence of the Bird-of-Prey through quantum teleportation, by actively transporting matter and energy from outside the envelope to the other side almost entirely unchanged and detectable only with the fastest and most sensitive instruments. Matter and energy produced inside the envelope, from sources like the ship's impulse engines, are temporarily stored within the field. An extremely small fraction of the total energy flux from local space, approximately 0.003 per cent, penetrates the cloak to allow for sub-light navigation.

An EM field produced by the emitter on the ship's exterior performs the actual cloaking by way of a complex spatial phasing of most incoming radiation. This phasing involves the short-range, almost instantaneous, quantum teleportation of radiation and particles through the cloak envelope as well as the ship itself. While the process is not 100 per cent efficient, it works well in the majority of situations a Bird-of-Prey is likely to encounter. The only major limitation it suffers from is that tachyons pass through the quantum teleportation envelope, and can therefore be used to detect the ship.

The cloaking generator occupies the outer areas of Deck 5L, below the bridge, with plasma conduits and other utilities straddling the photon torpedo launcher equipment built into Deck 6. Technically, the system uses two independent generators that are interconnected for redundancy. Each generator unit is built up from a set of seven major subassemblies, all of which are energized by superheated plasma from the dual warp cores.

The major components in a single cloaking system include a plasma manifold, plasma frequency conditioner, a cloak quantum teleport waveform accelerator, defensive shield energy diverter, emitter monitor, and the actual cloak field emitter. The final essential piece of equipment is a blast debris catcher ahead of the accelerator, which is designed to minimize damage to the plasma system if there is an internal structural failure.

The entire assembly measures 12.31 meters in length by 2.17 meters maximum diameter, and most of the equipment housings are currently forged from titanium and kellendide.

The plasma manifold delivers energy to the cloak from the warp engines, which are 100 meters aft. The plasma itself runs through conduits in the Deck 5L flooring. The system must be finely tuned at all times and in order to ensure the energy levels stay balanced, automatic gate valves control the flow of plasma through a lateral connector between the twin generators. The frequency conditioner adjusts the plasma energy to an optimal range for the quantum teleport subsystem, in much the same way that dilithium controls plasma frequencies in the engine core.

Within the teleport waveform accelerator, a series of 35 hollow energy raceways constructed of duranium proteanide speed up discrete plasma streams and synchronize their waveforms for eventual release through the emitter.

The shield energy diverter channels a portion of the system energy to the defensive shield grid embedded in

▶ **The bronze colored cloaking emitter runs around the perimeter of the bridge module.**

the hull plating, and can also create a shield layer through the cloak emitter, though this shielding is usually confined to a smaller envelope than that produced by the cloak and is nowhere near as effective as the full shield system used when the ship has decloaked.

The cloak emitter, a sealed tube 63.4 meters long and packed with temekenite waveguides and compression coils, essentially 'overloads' at an optimum frequency of 4265.2 pulses per second, continuously replenishing a thin wall space-time bubble around the ship.

The cloaking field has the obvious advantage of rendering the Bird-of-Prey virtually invisible in short-term stealth reconnaissance and combat missions. Most adversaries do not have the time nor the sensor capabilities to counter the cloak, and so most known shortcomings do not affect the statistical outcomes.

Subspace transmissions can be made from within the cloaking field, but they can be detected by enemy ships so when the cloaking device is active, it normally moves to silent running and all communications are banned. However, many commanders are willing to risk limited subspace communications when they are confident that

the ship is not in immediate danger of detection.

More seriously, the Bird-of-Prey must decloak in order to fire weapons. This results from the unique properties of the cloaking field, in that any beam or projectile weapon fired from inside the field will interact in unpredictable ways, from disappearing and rematerializing thousands of kilometers away, to dimensionally 'smearing' within the envelope, only to exit back inside and strike the ship. In practice, this means that any commander who is foolish enough to fire while cloaked is almost certain not to hit his target and is likely to end up destroying his own ship. As a result the designers of the Bird-of-Prey installed a software routine that disables the weapons systems while the ship is cloaked thus preventing more enthusiastic commanders from risking their crew's lives.

1 Plasma Manifold	**10** Axial Waveform Bypass Conduit
2 Warp Core Plasma Tap	**11** Photon Spill Window
3 Transverse Plasma Conduit	**12** Second-stage Teleport Waveform Accelerator
4 Plasma Conduit Scuff Pads	**13** Shield Energy Diverter
5 Plasma Connector	**14** Diverter Ion Sensor
6 Frequency Conditioner Inlet	**15** Cloaking Field Emitter Monitor
7 Frequency Conditioner	**16** Emitter Waveform Compressor
8 Blast Debris Shield	**17** Cloaking Field Emitter
9 First-stage Teleport Waveform Accelerator	**18** Structural Support Frames

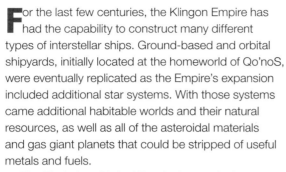
For the last few centuries, the Klingon Empire has had the capability to construct many different types of interstellar ships. Ground-based and orbital shipyards, initially located at the homeworld of Qo'noS, were eventually replicated as the Empire's expansion included additional star systems. With those systems came additional habitable worlds and their natural resources, as well as all of the asteroidal materials and gas giant planets that could be stripped of useful metals and fuels.

The *B'rel*-class Bird-of-Prey is the result of transforming those natural materials into a physical structure that could move between stars, one that surrounds and shields its crew. While built up of a number of seemingly incompatible alloy layers by a largely automated system, the basic framework and skin are deceptively simple in design. This has produced a ship that, once constructed and launched, can be repaired at most any Klingon-controlled yard and even those belonging to neighboring allies.

Many internal components are installed by robotic manipulators and remotely operated antigravs, but the majority of the critical systems that are to be used directly by warriors are installed manually and repeatedly checked throughout the construction period. It is a sign of trust and loyalty when a warrior crew accepts a new vessel, putting their lives in the hands of those who built it.

The preliminary shaping of a Bird-of-Prey involves seven separate major assembly jigs, two for the head, one for the neck, one for each wing, and two for the aft hull. Pre-formed frames and stringers are moved into place and gamma welded together, after which the alloy sheets for the inner pressure hull, also pre-formed, are electromechanically aligned and bonded.

The first layer is a 5.6cm thick sheet of *kar'dasnoth* attached to the open frame with *baakten* melt fasteners. All initial penetrations for conduits, structural reinforcements, waveguides, or other interlayer connections are made using computer-controlled beam cutters, and these openings will serve as templates for cutting through successive layers.

The second pressure hull layer is a 9.1cm shell of duranium and *baakten* composite that is bonded to the base *kar'dasnoth* shell. A 3mm sheet of conductive myltanine gadrium is sandwiched between the two; when this is energized by a narrow stream of matter-antimatter plasma, it permanently melts the surfaces together, intermixing the alloys to a depth of 0.8cm. Joins between plates are sealed the same way.

At this point, the pressure hull is some 12 times as strong as the first layer alone. The final structural layer is a 5.6cm shell of duranium titanide, which is energized and swirl-melted as before. This completes the basic hull, giving it a final thickness of 20.3cm.

For *B'rel*-class vessels constructed at the orbital yards at Dek'go'kor, major warp and impulse engine components such as reaction chambers and fuel tankage are secured to their interior locations while the hull is still open. The seven separate hull segments are integrated in a special microgravity fixture that keeps them in perfect three axis alignment while structural couplers are installed and welded together.

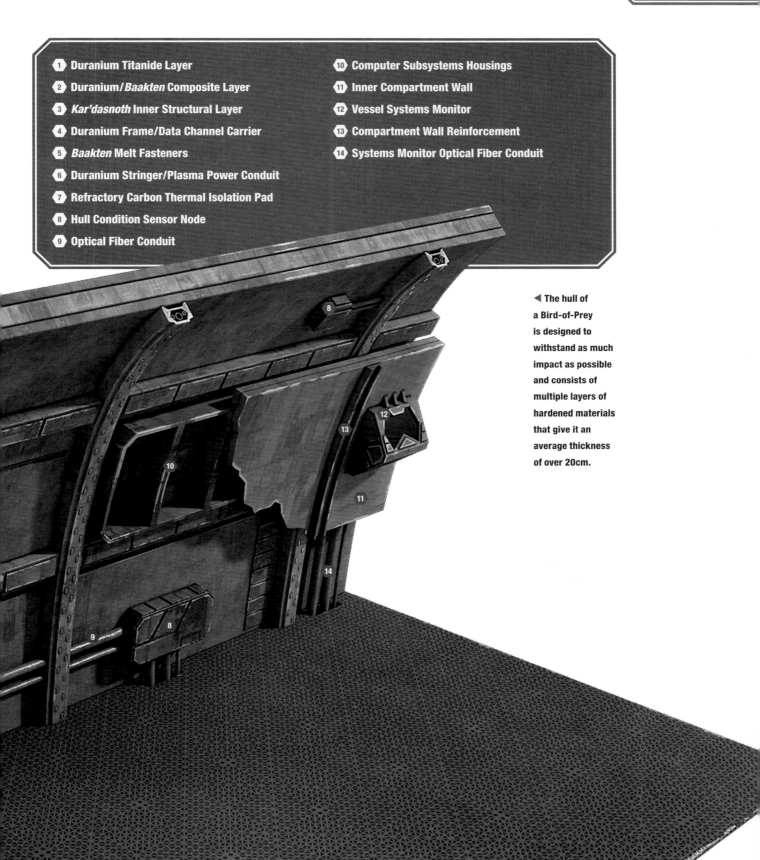

1. Duranium Titanide Layer
2. Duranium/*Baakten* Composite Layer
3. *Kar'dasnoth* Inner Structural Layer
4. Duranium Frame/Data Channel Carrier
5. *Baakten* Melt Fasteners
6. Duranium Stringer/Plasma Power Conduit
7. Refractory Carbon Thermal Isolation Pad
8. Hull Condition Sensor Node
9. Optical Fiber Conduit
10. Computer Subsystems Housings
11. Inner Compartment Wall
12. Vessel Systems Monitor
13. Compartment Wall Reinforcement
14. Systems Monitor Optical Fiber Conduit

◀ The hull of a Bird-of-Prey is designed to withstand as much impact as possible and consists of multiple layers of hardened materials that give it an average thickness of over 20cm.

The Bird-of-Prey is in a basic spaceworthy condition at this stage, but the Klingons now apply the armor layers that make it fit for combat. With each new alloy thickness, the ship gains strength, bringing it a step closer to full battle capability.

The first layer is a series of 17.65cm thick flanges and webs of *kar'dasnoth*, fastened to the duranium titanide hull. The webs provide an open standoff space that will slow fragments of projectile weapons. Structural integrity and defensive shield grid energy permeate the open volumes and minimize damage to the pressure hull.

The actual waveguides for the defensive shield are built into the second layer of armor plating—a 13.1cm layer of *ur hargol* and carbonitrium swirl-melted to the outer *kar'dasnoth* flanges.

The third armor layer consists of 7.9cm of foamed kovenium monoteserite, the same alloy used in the warp core. A solid layer of the metal over the entire ship would have proven too heavy for efficient impulse maneuvering, so a compromise was achieved by bonding together billions of hollow argon-filled kovenium microspheres. The result provides a balance between mass and impact and energy resistance.

Finally a 4.2cm layer of *kar'dasnoth* alloy is bonded to the hull. This layer, plus the 1.6cm surface ablation coating, are initial defense layers, designed to take hits and be replaced as combat repair items.

All armor layers require defensive grid and structural integrity field energy to be truly effective in countering enemy weapons, and few if any spacefaring cultures

have come up with a scheme that works better. In the Bird-of-Prey, two primary defensive shield generators are installed on Deck 5 in the aft hull, connected to emitters and waveguides that course through the entire vessel. A set of six smaller field amplifiers boost the shield coverage from Deck 6 in the head, under the bridge. Standard plasma power and data conduits service the shield generators, and the central computer monitors all possible hazards to the hull, not just under battle conditions.

Shield strength for different sectors of the ship can be ramped up and down depending on threat proximity, velocity, and incoming weapon energy, as well as available power and real-time ship maneuvers. Shield and structural integrity field generators can be overloaded, where the energy being dissipated is less than that being poured into the system from incoming weapons fire, explosions, or physical debris swarms.

Klingon military engineers have studied the combat experiences of Birds-of-Prey against numerous Starfleet, Romulan, Cardassian, Jem'Hadar, and other ships, often encountering weapons that initially seemed impossible to defeat. They have studied the data, made modifications, and continue to improve the defensive capabilities of the class.

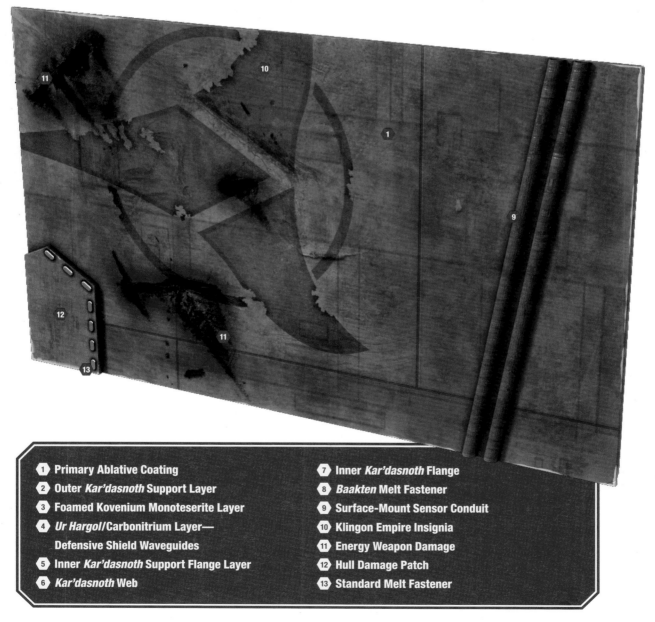

1. **Primary Ablative Coating**
2. **Outer *Kar'dasnoth* Support Layer**
3. **Foamed Kovenium Monoteserite Layer**
4. ***Ur Hargol*/Carbonitrium Layer— Defensive Shield Waveguides**
5. **Inner *Kar'dasnoth* Support Flange Layer**
6. ***Kar'dasnoth* Web**
7. **Inner *Kar'dasnoth* Flange**
8. ***Baakten* Melt Fastener**
9. **Surface-Mount Sensor Conduit**
10. **Klingon Empire Insignia**
11. **Energy Weapon Damage**
12. **Hull Damage Patch**
13. **Standard Melt Fastener**

The warp propulsion system of a *B'rel*-class vessel, and indeed of any ship in a proud Klingon battle group, is its warrior's heart. It is supplemented by a capable set of impulse engines for sub-light speeds, as well as reaction control thrusters that will pivot the Bird-of-Prey about like a soldier wielding a *bat'leth*. Guiding each ship through its moves are the Empire's most advanced computing and navigating systems, responding to the commander's orders promptly and efficiently.

The dual interconnected warp cores in Main Engineering blaze with high-temperature plasma, created by matter-antimatter reactions well understood by Klingon engineers for many centuries and enhanced by technical secrets appropriated from various space-faring cultures. Like Klingon physiology with its redundant organs, the Bird-of-Prey internal systems are duplicated and interconnected for the maximum number of options. A single warp core can move a Bird-of-Prey at FTL speeds if the other is offline. Impulse reactors can help get a ship to warp in a dire emergency. Backup fusion reactors can add engine power, and keep shields and other critical systems active.

Traversing tens or hundreds of lightyears is accomplished by the integration of redundant computer cores, mass memory devices, three-axis nav software, and short- and long-range external sensor bundles. Birds-of-Prey obtain constantly refreshed stellar position data by automated subspace beacons and compare that information with the sensor bundle input. Six crystal gyro rings and six backup micro-beam accelerometers transmit realtime attitude data to the main computer for routine flight calculations and battle-driven trajectories.

As part of their helm position training, Klingon warriors are expected to be able to orient the ship and fly between waypoints using nav computer sound cues alone with all visual screens blacked out.

Klingon ships rarely lose their way in the Galaxy.

Main Engineering is the largest single part of a B'rel-class Bird-of-Prey. It runs almost the entire width of the ship and spans the full height of Decks 3 to 6. It is 34.9m wide or abeam, 12.8m long fore to aft, and 15.6m tall. It is dominated by two large matter-antimatter reactors running through all four decks, almost the entire height of the ship. These twin reactors, commonly referred to as warp cores, are connected by a transverse plasma transfer conduit that combines energy from the cores and channels it to the warp wings.

The warp cores are controlled by a dedicated engineering computer node, which consists of four assemblies that are built into the decks and connected by an optical communications channel.

Main Engineering is the beating heart of the vessel, and is a center of constant activity, with warriors and equipment specialists keeping the hardware in perfect running order. Every component in this area, as well as in the adjoining impulse section, is expected to function under emergency conditions in ways even the original designers could only have considered for fleeting moments.

The twin warp cores work by combining streams of matter, in the form of deuterium, with streams of antimatter, in the form of anti-deuterium, to generate superheated plasma, which provides an enormously powerful energy source. The deuterium is held in a large insulated storage tank on Deck 4, which is refilled from other tanks on other decks, while the anti-deuterium is kept in anti-matter pods on Deck 6. The deuterium is injected directly into the reaction chambers at the top of each warp core, while the antimatter passes through antimatter manifolds that control the exact amount of antimatter in the system before it is injected into the bottom of the core.

Whenever matter and antimatter touch they create enormous amounts of energy, so it is vital that they only make contact inside the warp core where the reaction can be controlled. (At all other times, antimatter is kept suspended in a magnetic field that prevents it from coming into contact with any form of matter.) The warp engine harnesses a carefully controlled reaction to generate superheated plasma. This plasma is modified by dilithium crystals, which alter its frequency to make it suitable for use. The plasma is then channeled to a variety of ship's systems, the most important of which are the warp panels in the wings.

The sources of energy required to propel a

Bird-of-Prey are gathered far from its normal patrol routes, far from any large-scale battles for the glory of the Empire, and often long before some ships are even constructed. Production plants in different Klingon-held star systems toil to refine and chill down cryogenic deuterium and tritium, compressing and storing thousands of cubic meters of what was once the atmosphere of gas giant planets or the seas of more habitable worlds.

Other facilities burn vast quantities of those cryogenic ices in fusion reactors, powering exotic generators to change a small fraction of even more deuterium into antimatter. In a never-ending process, the Empire supplies the fuels every ship requires to become a living machine, to cross interstellar distances, and carry out the wishes of its commander.

Nowhere on a Bird-of-Prey is the power of matter and antimatter more evident than in Main Engineering. The twin cores are the central elements of a closed, pressurized system that funnels matter and antimatter together and distributes the vast amount of resulting energy from bow to stern. They work together, using gate valves and EM irises to ensure a proper balance of plasma flow from both reactor cores to the warp wings. If one of the cores isn't functioning properly, additional plasma can be distributed from the other core to keep the system operating. A Bird-of-Prey can function even if one of the cores is completely knocked out, though it will not be able to achieve high warp speeds.

The incredible energies produced in the reactors begin with semi-solid materials that are kept at −260°C. The central volume of matter is referred to as deuterium but is actually 92.57 per cent cryogenic deuterium mixed with 7.4 per cent tritium, another isotope of hydrogen, plus a final 0.03 per cent infusion of the pyroelectric crystal trigexite. It is maintained in an insulated storage tank on Deck 4, an immediate-use tank that is periodically refilled from similar tanks on other decks in the aft hull. Spiral mechanical pellet cutters and micro-force field emitters within the tank feed precise streams of deuterium to computer controlled pumps, and then through conduits to the matter injectors high up on Deck 3.

The antimatter, in the form of anti-deuterium, is stored in a series of magnetically-shielded containment pods in Main Engineering that slide into racks on the floor of Deck 6. Like a great deal of the Bird-of-Prey's structure, the pods are made from machined and gamma-welded duranium titanide.

WARP CORE

The Bird-of-Prey's twin warp cores are constructed of some the strongest materials ever devised for starships. They are each 16.38m tall and 7.26m in diameter at their widest points, and are attached to the vessel frame with twelve momentum conditioners—shock absorbers—that allow each reactor to 'float' within open holes in Decks 3, 4, 5, and 6.

Each core is fabricated as two major subassemblies, the reinforcing framework and the matter-antimatter reactor itself. The reinforcing frame, made from varying proportions of *kar'dasnoth* and *baakten*, relies on a combination of compression and tension members to hold the reactor together. The two metals—variants of densified tritanium—are blended in vapor-deposition furnaces, creating tight atomic matrices that are somewhat brittle, but exceedingly strong.

The reactor walls are built with a similar vapor-deposition technique from multiple alternating layers of *genn'thok* and *ur hargol* and hardened by exposure to controlled plasma detonations. The hexagonal photon spill 'windows' are created during the initial fabrication steps by altering the atomic structure, similar to transparent aluminum, to allow 0.000013 of the visible spectrum to pass through.

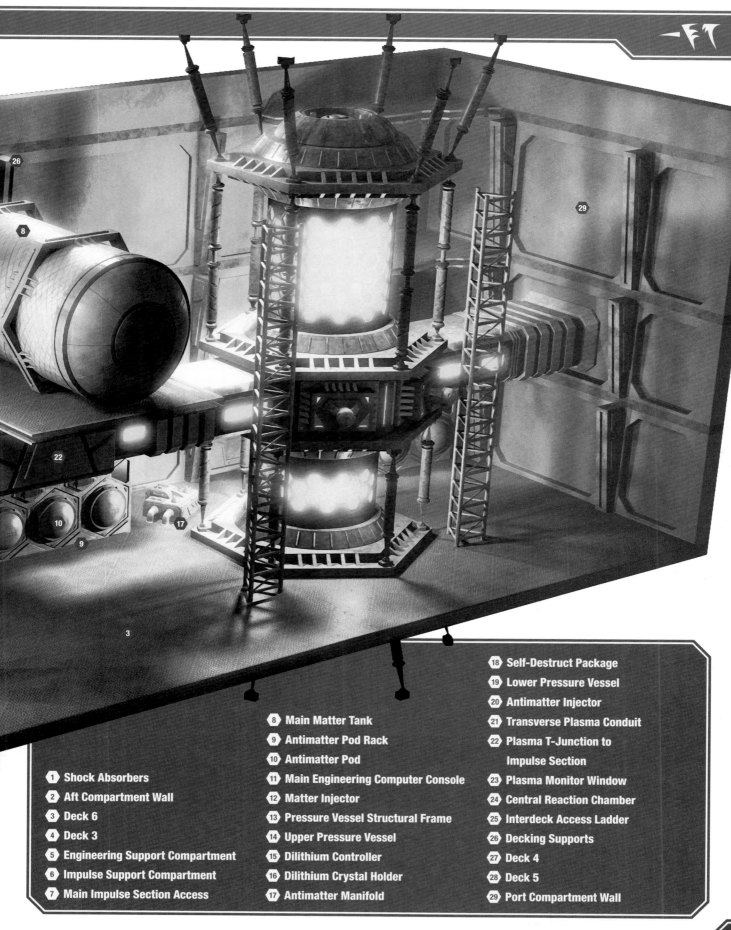

1 Shock Absorbers
2 Aft Compartment Wall
3 Deck 6
4 Deck 3
5 Engineering Support Compartment
6 Impulse Support Compartment
7 Main Impulse Section Access

8 Main Matter Tank
9 Antimatter Pod Rack
10 Antimatter Pod
11 Main Engineering Computer Console
12 Matter Injector
13 Pressure Vessel Structural Frame
14 Upper Pressure Vessel
15 Dilithium Controller
16 Dilithium Crystal Holder
17 Antimatter Manifold

18 Self-Destruct Package
19 Lower Pressure Vessel
20 Antimatter Injector
21 Transverse Plasma Conduit
22 Plasma T-Junction to Impulse Section
23 Plasma Monitor Window
24 Central Reaction Chamber
25 Interdeck Access Ladder
26 Decking Supports
27 Deck 4
28 Deck 5
29 Port Compartment Wall

◥ The warp engines use antimatter in the form of anti-deuterium which is stored in 20 pods that prevent it from coming into contact with normal matter.

▶ ANTIMATTER PODS

The antimatter pods have been designed to withstand most physical shocks from battle damage in the engineering section, typically from falling or shattered equipment, and even most short-duration energy weapons. It is ironic that while a great many redundant safety measures have been built into the antimatter pods, the racks in which they sit have been designed to hold the primary self-destruct explosive packages. [See page 91]

The *B'rel*-class uses a total of 20 antimatter pods in Main Engineering, which are distributed among two six-pod and two four-pod racks. If they are needed, additional tanks can be stored in the engineering support areas further forward on Deck 6, depending on the mission. Both rack types are 3.87m tall, about twice the height of a warrior; the large rack is 4.92m wide and the smaller one is 3.34m wide.

Pods can be installed and extracted by mechanical lifts or antigravs. Like the pods, the racks are also fitted with magnetic isolation valves and conduits that prevent the antimatter from coming into contact with normal matter.

1. Impact Armor Cap
2. Structural End Plate
3. Tension Bar
4. Rack Cradle Alignment Plate
5. Duranium Titanide Tank
6. Cradle Scuff Plate
7. Magnetic Transfer Conduit
8. Anti-Grav Transport Lock
9. Pod Reinforcement Plate
10. Magnetic Vacuum Vent

1. Pod Rack Structural Frame
2. Antimatter Pod
3. Self-Destruct Package
4. Pod Support Cradle
5. Frame Reinforcement Plates
6. Pod Status Monitor

They measure 1.56m in diameter and 2.92m long and are heavily lined with Type-III neodium-gallinide, which magnetically repels the anti-deuterium at least 2.3cm, preventing it from touching the inner walls of the pod and therefore causing an uncontrolled matter-antimatter explosion.

Each pod has a pellet cutter at the aft end that uses a shielded micro-force field maniuplator to isolate tiny packets of anti-deuterium, into magnetically contained pellets, approximately 6mm in diameter, that it pushes through the system.

The anti-deuterium pellets do not flow directly to the antimatter injectors but instead pass through a set of intermediate manifolds, two per warp core, which include additional magnetic gate valves and mass monitors. Antimatter is a dangerous substance under the best of conditions, and even more so in a combat vessel where the smallest containment breach can spell disaster. As such, all pods, mag-lined conduits, and connectors are equipped with superconducting coils that will continue to provide shielding for 35 minutes if power to the system is cut.

During normal flight operations, the antimatter manifolds apply pulsed magnetic fields to send the anti-deuterium pellets through one last set of conduits before they reach the injectors just below Deck 6.

Ideally, the reactant flows and injector firings are balanced in both warp cores through constant sensor monitoring and adjustments by both the Main Engineering computer node and the central computer.

▼ The antimatter pods are stored in racks in engineering that are connected to the engines and allow antimatter to be fed into the system.

In practice, however, the propulsion control software is constantly chasing slight imbalances that are felt as occasional but annoying vibrations. In combat, if a warp core is damaged but still operating, the total fuel flow system does what it can to smooth out the plasma going to the wing warp drives, weapons, and general power network.

The temperature and pressure of the plasma in the reactor is regulated by precisely controlling the flow rates of the matter and antimatter. The frequency of the plasma is controlled by four dilithium controllers, which ring the middle section of each core. Each controller covers a small penetration in the reactor and contains a removable assembly that securely holds a large piece of dilithium crystal into the plasma stream.

The crystals extend into the core, where they're bathed in the plasma, and as the plasma passes between the four crystals in each core they alter its frequency. Through a set of actuators the clamp assembly can adjust the crystal angle and rotation to reach the best frequency level for a particular flight regime.

Complete control over warp velocities is a complex numerical dance as the Main Engineering computer node commands all eight crystal clamps, coordinates the reactor temperatures and pressures, and triggers the proper warp wing energizing sequence.

The modified plasma stream passes from the warp cores into the transverse plasma transfer

1. Antimatter Inlet Conduits
2. Manifold Casing Reinforcements
3. Waste Heat Controlled Release Port
4. Antimatter Temperature Monitor
5. Antimatter Flow Monitor
6. System Power Indicator
7. Contingency Flow Redirect Port
8. System Status Indicators
9. Antimatter Sample Port
10. Maintenance Lift Fixture
11. Magnetic Field Test Port

▶ The antimatter manifolds provide precise control over the amount of antimatter that passes into the warp engines.

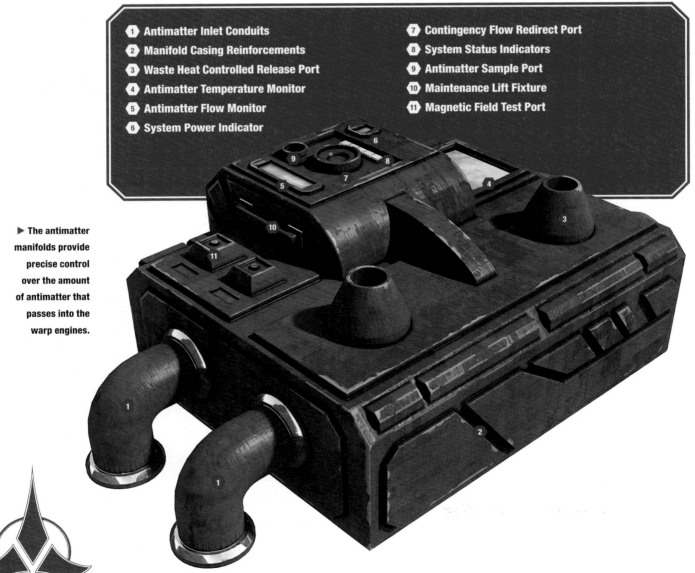

▶▲ The antimatter
manifolds (two
per warp core)
feed a stream of
antimatter pellets
suspended in
carefully controlled
micro force fields
into the bottom of
the warp reactors.

conduit for distribution throughout the ship. The conduit itself runs to the warp wings but it also incorporates a series of six medium and 30 smaller EPS (electroplasma) energy taps, which are channeled to every part of the ship for basic power. The transverse conduit contains a number of visual inspection ports similar to the hexagonal photon spill versions in the cores, used for general confirmation of the flow and intensity of the plasma.

The ability to divert superheated plasma to any part of the ship's energy system gives the Bird-of-Prey a unique advantage over other faster-than-light starships.

Four sets of computer-controlled gate valves, each consisting of a pair of metallic composite doors and an electromagnetic iris, can be opened and closed to channel plasma to the warp wings, disruptors, impulse engines, and life-support systems, usually prioritized in that order.

The amount of plasma used in each system can also be adjusted, depending on the condition of the core. The warp drive is deemed more important than the impulse or sublight engines, since the warp wings can also propel the ship at fractional warp values if necessary.

If one or both cores are running at less than optimal output for any reason, including battle damage, the system can still measure and balance the energy and pressure in the plasma conduits that head to the wings.

If necessary, the EM irises can constrict tightly and then open in precise cycles to generate high plasma pressure and high temperature if the cores are not running properly. The technique does not work for

long periods and is wasteful of fuel, but can be useful in a crisis.

At the center of the transverse plasma conduit, there is a T-section diverter that can send plasma to the impulse engines. This is a backup system that is activated only if the impulse fusion reactors cannot access their regular energy source, but it compensates for several of the most likely forms of impulse engine failure. The reverse is also possible under extraordinary conditions, where energy from the impulse chambers can assist in warp flight through the same giant conduit. [See page 70]

All of the central reactor hardware is surrounded by structures that protect it from most weapon hits, plus all of the necessary utilities to keep them running. The spaceframe elements enveloping this section are reinforced by the decking and by vertical and horizontal support members, all of which are fabricated from alloys of duranium and titanium and varying proportions of embedded nanocarbon whiskers.

The pressure hull around Main Engineering is almost twice the thickness of that on the rest of the ship. The standard hull thickness is 20.33cm whereas in Engineering it is 32.71cm. The outer armor layer is also reinforced and the standard thickness of 44.45cm is given an additional kinetic and beam weapon ablator layer 12.32cm.

The total physical impact hull—without defensive energy shields—measures some 89.48cm thick, nearly a meter of solid matter. When this is added to the spaceframe member thickness of 26.27cm, in places the overall protection reaches as much as 1.15m.

The need for the additional armor is two-fold; while the alloy layers are designed to stop incoming weapons fire, they are also in place to limit explosion effects from internal causes. The walls and frames help contain reactor plasma breaches, while the large transverse plasma conduit opens to space and bleeds off pressure through the ventral wing vents. Any amount of containment helps in most breach scenarios, and provides valuable time to fix the situation or prepare for escape from the vessel.

Adjacent engineering support rooms contain vital subsystems, including electrohydraulic pumps, pressurized gas spheres and cylinders, plasma sampling and monitoring gear, and sensor processors. The support rooms, which are rather hot and cramped, occupy the twin narrow tail pieces of the hull to the port and starboard of the impulse section, and share a number of subsystems with the impulse engines.

Most of these subsystems on one side are interconnected with their twins on the opposite side and can all be shut down and isolated or left active as needed. Access doors and hatches on Decks 4, 5, and 6 lead into the support rooms and allow for transfer of swappable machine components and supply tanks manually or by antigrav.

Each door contains safety locks to prevent opening if the compartment beyond is damaged and open to space. Command overrides of the door locking mechanisms, emergency force fields, and

▶ **Each reactor uses four dilithium crystals which are housed around the outside of the warp core.**

hostile environment suits come into play if repairs or rescue situations warrant. Crew movement between decks, either in the support compartments or in Main Engineering itself, is accomplished by ladder wells. The largest of these are three triangular ladders close to the warp reactors that allow for quick inspections and equipment swapouts.

Thick bundles of optical fiber and carbon data ribbon are built into the walls and decking, and connect to sensors that record all aspects of engine operation and environmental conditions, transmit equipment programs and activation commands, and relay all relevant information to the central computer and the bridge.

Redundant engineering computer nodes are installed in hardened casings just outside of the armored space on Deck 6. These nodes, equipped with emergency subspace beacons, preserve duplicate data records in the event of a catastrophic failure. Unless the casings are hit directly by weapons fire, there is a good chance they will survive being ejected into space or thrown about a planetary surface.

Besides the data and power conduits, other piping networks transport gases and liquids among the various major engine assemblies and support gear. The largest fluid pipes replenish the cryogenic matter tanks, and smaller ones move coolant, liquified breathing gases, and hardware cleaning compounds.

1. Dilithium Crystal
2. *Genn'thok* Pressure Pad
3. *Ur Hargol* Articulated Control Arms
4. Carbonitrium Pressure Plug
5. Pressure Relief Ports
6. External Plug Cap

DILITHIUM

Dilithium crystals degrade over time, coating the inner reactor walls with thin layers of atoms and requiring frequency recalibration every 3900 operating hours. Once thought impossible, dilithium can undergo recrystallization using reclaimed materials and quantum scaffolding. Crystals are tested on board the ship and reconstructed if necessary, or handed off to an Empire shipyard during maintenance layovers.

▲ Dilithium plays a vital role in 'tuning' the matter-antimatter reaction. Huge amounts of Klingon dilithium come from the mines on Rura Penthe.

The Bird-of-Prey achieves warp flight using a different system of energized alloys from other ships in the IKDF fleet. Most civilizations that are capable of faster than light travel use circular or oval rings of space-bending metals and composites. The familiar 'warp coils'—housed in stand-off nacelles or incorporated within a starship hull—warp space and provide propulsion when they are exposed to high energy plasma.

Early Klingon, Vulcan, and Romulan vessels used this system to make their way through interstellar space, employing a variety of cryogenic fuels and antimatter to achieve greater and greater speeds and distances. While plasma reactions had originally been triggered directly within the nacelles, advances in pumping super hot plasma from remote—and protected—engines allowed for larger, more powerful systems. Magnetically lined conduits could be routed through different ship structures. Crystalline materials such as ikemenite, faslonite, and dilithium became standards for regulating the furious energies and smoothing out the plasma frequencies within the core.

Design engineers within the Imperial Klingon

Defense Forces, with ship commanders taking an active role in deciding what systems were to be installed in *their* ships, experimented early in the 22nd century with reshaping the usual nacelle configuration for new classes of fast, stealthy attack vessels.

It was determined that the sequential energizing of warp alloys did not necessarily require the 'coils' to be coils at all, but the alloys could be compacted into flat sheets. Beginning with Klingon vessels of the 2120s, the energized warp wing was born, leading to the development of the 23rd-century *B'rel*-class Bird-of-Prey with its imposing bird shape.

In the *B'rel*-class, plasma produced in the twin warp cores is allowed to fill and pressurize the central horizontal conduits that lead to the wings, through penetrations in the engineering hull on Deck 5. Each central conduit has a variable aperture duct, which works in concert with the wing hinge to provide different amounts and pressures of plasma to the warp system depending on the flight mode—liftoff/landing, cruise, and attack.

The first component the plasma encounters in the wing is the plasma manifold and pumping inlet. From a cold-start condition, the manifold and

▼ **The concept of the warp wing was pioneered in the 22nd-century Bird-of-Prey— the *B'rel* class refined the design.**

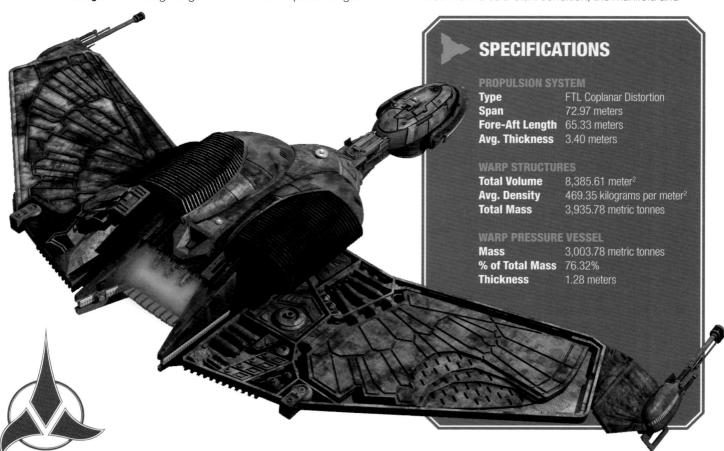

SPECIFICATIONS

PROPULSION SYSTEM
Type	FTL Coplanar Distortion
Span	72.97 meters
Fore-Aft Length	65.33 meters
Avg. Thickness	3.40 meters

WARP STRUCTURES
Total Volume	8,385.61 meter^2
Avg. Density	469.35 kilograms per meter^2
Total Mass	3,935.78 metric tonnes

WARP PRESSURE VESSEL
Mass	3,003.78 metric tonnes
% of Total Mass	76.32%
Thickness	1.28 meters

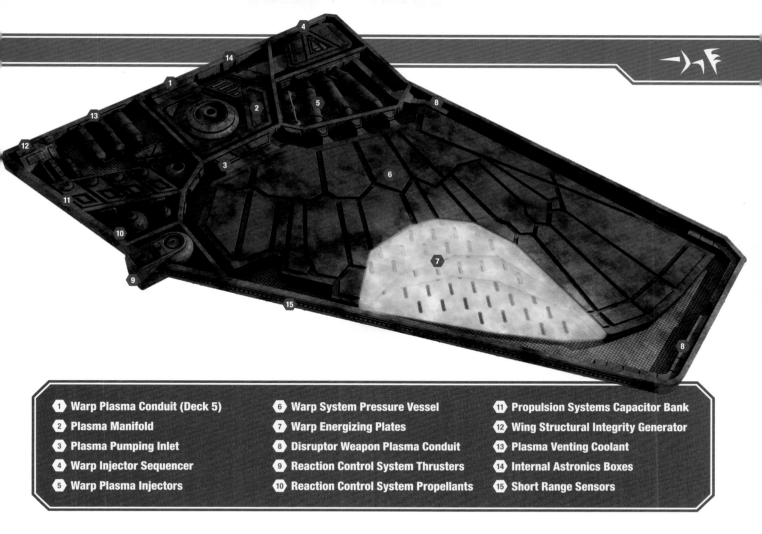

1 Warp Plasma Conduit (Deck 5)

2 Plasma Manifold

3 Plasma Pumping Inlet

4 Warp Injector Sequencer

5 Warp Plasma Injectors

6 Warp System Pressure Vessel

7 Warp Energizing Plates

8 Disruptor Weapon Plasma Conduit

9 Reaction Control System Thrusters

10 Reaction Control System Propellants

11 Propulsion Systems Capacitor Bank

12 Wing Structural Integrity Generator

13 Plasma Venting Coolant

14 Internal Astronics Boxes

15 Short Range Sensors

pumping inlet send plasma to the system pressure vessel to 65,000 kilopascals (641 atmospheres) and 1,750,000K. The manifold then shuts the inlet and switches to supplying the injector sequencer and plasma injectors. Normally there are three injectors firing fore to aft, creating a repeating, traveling warp field wave that imparts a lightening of the apparent mass and forward motion to the ship. This pressure vessel is the toughest single part of the Bird-of-Prey, and is constructed of interlocking slabs of kovenium monoteserite, a material found in quantity in a handful of systems in the Klingon Empire.

All parts of the plasma system that are exposed to high pressures and temperatures have some amount of kovenium monoteserite in them, as Klingon engineers have discovered that this material helps to reinforce the structural integrity of the ship on the sub-atomic scale when it is connected to the structural integrity field generator.

Like other vessels that use dual warp fields, the Bird-of-Prey achieves controlled, balanced flight by making minor alterations to the strength of each field. Incredibly precise computer instructions control the shape of each field by firing the plasma injectors at different rates. Essentially, to turn right the pilot

reduces the strength of the right warp field.

The wing warp system, as part of the overall Klingon predilection for redundancy and multiple options, is also capable of propelling the ship at sub-light velocities.

A portion of the warp plasma generated by the cores is routed to the wingtip disruptor weapons, which are typically fired at sub-light speeds with the wings in the lowered position. At the lowest angle, the hinged plasma conduit between the hull and the wing closes almost completely, creating the optimum plasma pressure for disruptor firing. Two main conduits within the wing, one a tap off the injector sequencer and the other a tap off the warp pressure vessel, converge on the wingtip to feed the disruptor.

Other sub-systems housed in the wing include a pair of main reaction control system thrusters per wing and their propellant tanks. If rapid venting of drive plasma is required, a set of cryogenic helium tanks is also available to cool the plasma outlets just below the plasma manifold. The last large sub-system encompasses a bank of electroplasma capacitors that services the structural integrity field generator and all other astronic systems, sensors, and servo mechanisms.

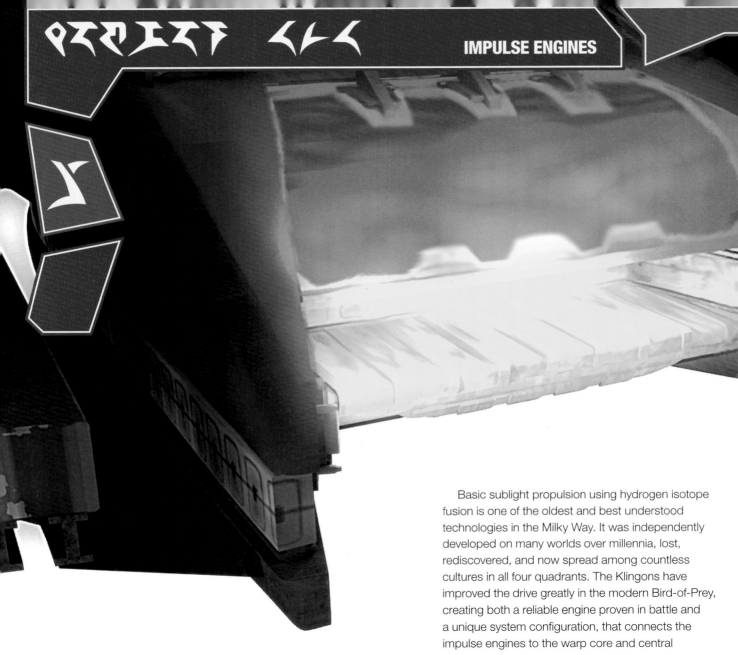

Basic sublight propulsion using hydrogen isotope fusion is one of the oldest and best understood technologies in the Milky Way. It was independently developed on many worlds over millennia, lost, rediscovered, and now spread among countless cultures in all four quadrants. The Klingons have improved the drive greatly in the modern Bird-of-Prey, creating both a reliable engine proven in battle and a unique system configuration, that connects the impulse engines to the warp core and central plasma conduit.

The *B'rel*-class operates 14 individual impulse engines, each consisting of an initial fusion reaction chamber, space-time driver and mass reduction coils, and vectored exhaust nozzle. Each engine is equipped with two cryogenic deuterium-only tanks, which are replenished from additional storage tanks in the port and starboard tail extensions. The large tank in Main Engineering can also be used, though the addition of tritium and trigexite necessitates changes in the reactor ignition power levels.

Four large engine assemblies are mounted on Deck 4, and eight smaller units are mounted below this on Deck 6, all just aft of Main Engineering and the twin warp cores. The two engine groups are separated by a large external gap at the end of what

Unless it is traveling faster than the speed of light, the Bird-of-Prey relies on its impulse engines, which use a series of nuclear fusion reactors to generate the power needed to lighten its mass and push it through space or through a planet's atmosphere.

While they may not be as powerful as the warp engines, the Bird-of-Prey's impulse engines are considered to be the ship's most important single system, even above the cloak and weapons. Without reliable impulse flight there would be no way to engage enemy vessels or reach planets and asteroids to deliver raiding parties. The Empire has worked long and hard to perfect its engines alone and in secret, benefiting from deals with allies, or stealing technology when it suited their purposes.

would be Deck 5. Each group is isolated from the other and accessed through different sets of armored pressure doors. The main entrance to the impulse engine rooms are hatches in Main Engineering. The hatch on Deck 4 is immediately aft of the deuterium storage tank, while the separate engine assembly on Deck 6 is reached through a hatch between the racks of antimatter pods.

The impulse engineering space is 24.3m wide for both sections; the Deck 4 area is 5.3m tall while the Deck 6 section is shorter at 3.8m.

Unlike the constant maintenance activity needed to keep the warp cores running efficiently, the impulse sections require only occasional monitoring and repair inspections outside of battle conditions. The Deck 4 propulsion units are designed specifically for mass lightening and forward flight, while the eight lower engines not only provide forward flight motion but have the added capability of vertical take-off and landing. Two additional downward-venting engines are located on Deck 4 near the ship's neck section.

In the nominal flight mode, a continuous stream of cryogenic deuterium is gasified, injected into the toroidal reaction chamber, and crushed into a blazing ring by dual-mode laser and magnetic pinch emitters to achieve fusion. The initial energy pulses must come

from either the warp plasma network or banks of tetrapolymer power cells, but once the fusion cycle stabilizes, the reactor will jump past the 'break even' point and produce more energy than it takes to compress the stream.

This system, like the warp cores, will continue to work as long as fuel is available. Fusion plasma is spiraled off and channeled into the space-time driver coils, which push a low-level subspace field through the ship's entire structure. This field lightens the apparent mass and propels the ship forward. It is analogous to the motive force created by the warp wing alloys, but at much lower energies.

The power generated by the warp reactor is still nearly a million times greater than that released by the impulse fusion chambers, necessary to drive the ship across the faster-than-light barrier. Any exhaust products from the fusion reaction, primarily waste heat and gases, are vented through the vectored exhaust nozzles. As with most impulse systems currently in use, the exhaust does little to actually move the vessel, as the driver coils do all of the actual pushing and pulling through the continuum. Under stealth conditions, especially when the vessel is cloaked, the majority of the exhaust products can be stored temporarily in the nozzle section.

▲ The Bird-of-Prey's impulse engines are used for maneuvering at sublight speeds whether that is in open space or a planetary atmosphere.

IMPULSE ENGINE ROOM

► The main
impulse engine
room is on Deck 4
and contains four
fusion reactor
assemblies.

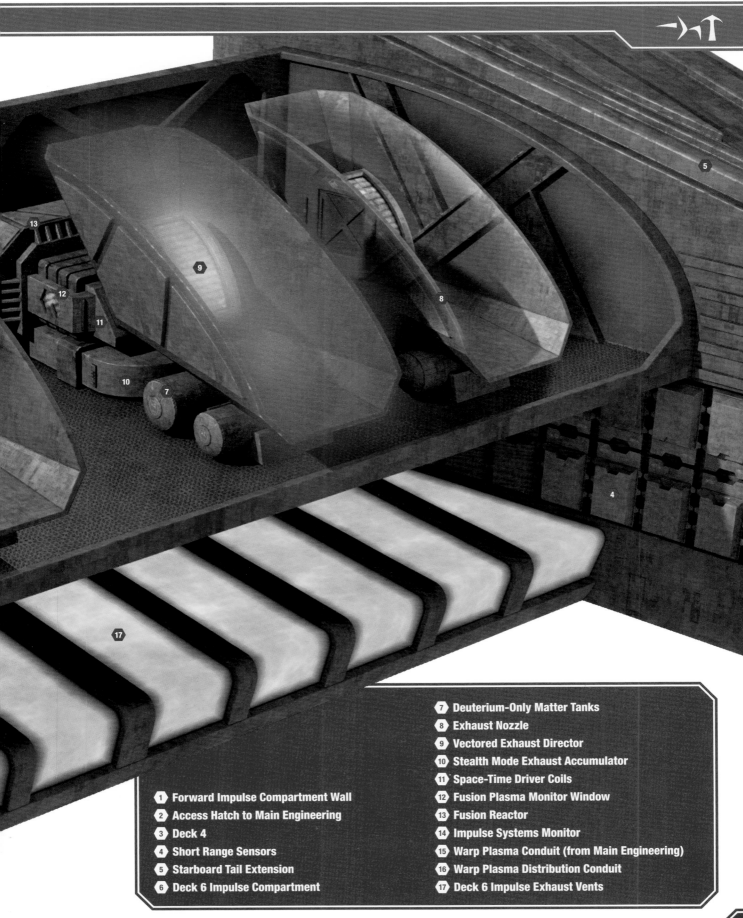

1 Forward Impulse Compartment Wall
2 Access Hatch to Main Engineering
3 Deck 4
4 Short Range Sensors
5 Starboard Tail Extension
6 Deck 6 Impulse Compartment

7 Deuterium-Only Matter Tanks
8 Exhaust Nozzle
9 Vectored Exhaust Director
10 Stealth Mode Exhaust Accumulator
11 Space-Time Driver Coils
12 Fusion Plasma Monitor Window
13 Fusion Reactor
14 Impulse Systems Monitor
15 Warp Plasma Conduit (from Main Engineering)
16 Warp Plasma Distribution Conduit
17 Deck 6 Impulse Exhaust Vents

▼ **Two impulse engines on Deck 4 near the front of the main body of the ship are used to control the ship's movement in the Y axis.**

The coils can be configured for flight in any direction, making the Bird-of-Prey highly maneuverable in space and during planetside flight operations. The key to controlling the ship's motion at sublight speeds lies in the triggering order of the coils and the plasma intensity sent through them. Both factors—translated into heading and velocity—are controlled directly from the bridge by the helm officer. Preprogrammed maneuvers, particularly in battle, are selectable at the helm, with manual control returned to the helm officer when conditions allow or when overrides are called for.

Impulse flight is usually limited to one-third of c, the speed of light. This is about 100,000 kilometers, or roughly 50,000 kellicams per second. Extended travel at this velocity or higher leads to a time distortion effect and requires resetting of the ship's chronometers. As most starships of different cultures track relativistic changes through internal computer routines and sensor inputs, this is generally more of an annoyance than a true operational issue. Warp flight eliminates most time-based problems, though the *B'rel, K'vort,* and *Vor'cha* class ships continue to experience some small temporal differences while traveling at fractional warp factors, essentially sublight flight using warp engines.

Klingon propulsion designers have taken the concept of redundant and alternative systems to the extreme with the physical connection of the impulse engines to their warp counterparts. Depending on the situation, opening and shutting plasma flows in either direction could save a ship.

Bird-of-Prey commanders often need to become masters of their ship's engine systems and to be aware of the many options available to them if they are to stay in the fight and triumph against enormous odds. Most are privately grateful for the help from the central computer, but they and their engineer warriors learn which options to choose through long experience.

One scenario, not considered likely but validated in numerous simulations, involves assisting a failing warp engine system to at least cross the Warp 1 threshold. If going faster than light becomes a survival measure, all twelve impulse reactors, if functioning, are run at 155%, with their energy diverted to the warp plasma conduit. Crossing Warp 1 requires a considerable amount of power, but once over, the power required to maintain low warp drops off slightly.

The more likely scenario involves using the warp cores to power the impulse driver coils. This may occur if the fusion toroids are out of commission, or if their output is seriously degraded, with other parts of the system unharmed. The warp plasma is channeled through the T-conduit in Main Engineering, into distribution junctions in the impulse compartments—one on Deck 4 and one on Deck 6 —and finally into the individual impulse engine units. If everything flows correctly, the helm will have sublight flight control. If some of the driver coils are damaged, as has happened on the *Rotarran*, those units are isolated and the time to reach a desired speed will take longer. Prior to invoking the complex protocols for using the escape pods, a commander and his crew will make use of any opportunity to regroup, repair, and return to battle. The Klingon motto shown opposite illustrates this perfectly:

1. Deuterium Injector
2. Ship Support Fixture
3. Transverse Structural Member
4. Structural Reinforcement
5. Scuff Pads
6. Fusion Initiator Test Port
7. Vessel Shock Pad Fixture
8. Fusion Initiator Capacitor Bank
9. Fusion Reaction Chamber Housing
10. Overboard Heat Dump
11. Fusion Initiator Mag Pump
12. Vectored Exhaust Nozzle

▶ The forward impulse engines have the same basic components as the main impulse engines and combine a fusion reactor with mass-lightening coils.

ghoSlaHbe'chugh Duj may' yaH yIchenmoH HoS HutlhchughnISwI'mey qach QaD yIchenmoH jagh DajeylaHbe'chugh batlh yIHegh.	If the ship cannot proceed, create a battle station. If the disruptors lack energy, create a protected structure. If you cannot defeat the enemy, die honorably.

ᏰᏝᏋᎠᏋᏁ

▲▼ A series of four RCS engines are located in an assembly on each wing. In each case, two thrusters point up and two point down.

The Reaction Control System (RCS) thrusters on the *B'rel*-class Bird-of-Prey are a set of four main microfusion engines and four smaller vernier or trim engines. The RCS system is designed exclusively for use during impulse flight, specifically in aid of combat maneuvers involving high rotational rates about the ship's center of gravity.

These engines are housed in swappable modules installed on the trailing edges of the warp wings.

Unlike most other starships, the Bird-of-Prey does not normally use its RCS thrusters for small-scale maneuvers such as those encountered in dockings or surface landings. Instead low three-axis translational rates from 5.5 down to 0.3 meters per second are handled by precisely energizing the impulse engine fields. The RCS engines only aid in aligning the ship's rotational attitude during these movements, before station docking clamps are activated or before the landing gear makes contact with the ground.

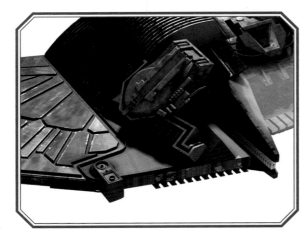

The large primary RCS engines are each 1.94 meters tall, and consist of a central microfusion chamber and associated fuel and power system housing, and an expansion nozzle. In each warp wing module, one thruster fires upward and another downward. The nozzle, which is made of *baakten* alloy lined with a 3.2cm mixed ablative layer of carbonitrium and *ur hargol*, measures 72.1cm across and 59.3cm high. It is attached to the motor body, which is 134.7cm tall and constructed of directionally strengthened duranium krellide. The entire assembly is attached to the wing module structure at two hardpoints.

The hexagonal microfusion section houses a toroidal, 62cm-across plasma pinch chamber. Deuterium is fed into this in the same way it is to the impulse engines. However, the RCS engines don't use space-time driver coils, and rely on pure fusion exhaust alone to provide the necessary thrust. The engine is throttleable, and can produce between 250 and 4300 metric tonnes of thrust.

The engine subsystems include a plasma power coupling, deuterium flow valves, computer control and sensor connections, and an overpressure relief vent. The plasma coupling taps into the ship's basic power network, providing the energy necessary to initiate the microfusion reaction in the torus.

A set of capacitors nearby in the wing are available as backup power sources.

The deuterium fuel used by the engines is stored in two pressurized tanks that are next to the RCS modules in the warp wings. It passes through a series of gate valves and conduits before it

1. Microfusion Chamber Housing
2. Thrust Expansion Nozzle
3. Nozzle Flange Cover
4. Chamber Temperature Sensor
5. Chamber Overpressure Bleed Vent
6. Chamber Maintenance Plate
7. Computer Control/Sensor Data Conduit
8. Plasma Power Coupling
9. Thruster Structural Attachment
10. Waste Heat Radiator
11. Deuterium Feeder Conduit

reaches the primary thrusters in semi-slush form.

The RCS engines are controlled and monitored by a combined optical and carbon ribbon data bundle that is connected to both the Main Engineering computer node on Deck 6 and the engineering station on the bridge.

The overpressure vent is opened normally during routine RCS shutdown events, after a series of maneuvers or for maintenance. The vent conduit ejects surplus energy into space through a non-propulsive port.

The vernier engines, used in either combination with the main thrusters or alone, are 71 per cent scaled copies of their larger cousins. The subsystem connections are virtually identical, and the output can be throttled between 15 and 190 metric tonnes of thrust.

Thruster operation is normally activated by combat maneuvering subroutines in the central computer, which are in turn activated by commands from the helm officer.

Direct fusion thrust from the RCS nozzles has a slight advantage over impulse engine motive power alone in that it can overcome a small lag from the space-time driver fields, which experienced helm officers sometimes criticize as "rubbery." This can get the Bird-of-Prey moving in the desired axis as much as 2–3 seconds quicker depending on the relative speed and aspect of the target.

Programmed maneuvers in the computer are coordinated with the ship's subspace gyro system, accelerometer grid, and short range targeting sensors. These trigger thruster firings with the quickest possible system reaction times.

In benign situations such as space station or planetary approach, thruster firings are balanced for smooth rotations. In combat, however, all rate limiters are turned off, and the Bird-of-Prey can—and does—pitch and roll as required to survive. Violent movements can be felt even with inertial dampeners at full power.

During planetary landings, particularly at active military staging areas, the main RCS thrusters are deactivated when the ship gets within 230 meters of the ground and the verniers take over the fine-tuning of the approach to minimize thermal effects in the touchdown area.

The most constant threat faced by a Bird-of-Prey isn't an enemy vessel but the damage that could be inflicted by specs of dust. Like all vessels traveling at the kind of velocities needed to traverse interstellar space, if the Bird-of-Prey collided with dust, cometary emissions, micrometeroids and even gasses it would penetrate the hull causing catastrophic damage that would kill the crew in seconds.

These particles pose a continuous hazard to navigation, beginning with relative velocities as low as 20,000 kellicams per hour—some 40,000 kilometers per hour. The problem becomes even greater at warp speed. The Bird-of-Prey's on-board navigational computers will automatically plot a course around large objects such as planets or even asteroids, but the only effective way of dealing with small particles is to clear them out of the ship's path.

Various spacefaring cultures have used electromagnetics and radiative subspace devices to build barriers ahead of their ships, effectively driving particles away from the flight path. Some of these deflector fields have a very long range. This is necessary at warp factors as high as warp 9 where the ship is traveling many times the speed of light and yet must move particles away before the ship reaches them.

Many spacefaring cultures use multi-tonne coils and dishes to create a sweeping deflector path. The *B'rel*-class employs a combination of smaller fields generated by the plasma-powered warp wing, the close-in field emitted by the defensive shields, plus a more powerful

DEFENSIVE SHIELD DEFLECTOR

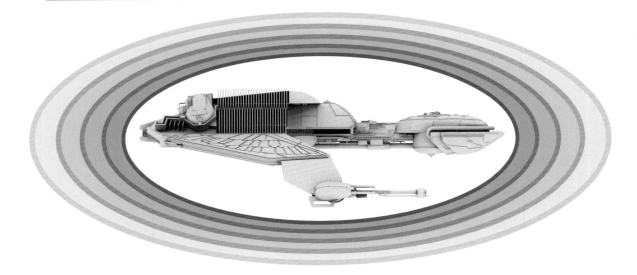

CENTRAL DEFLECTOR

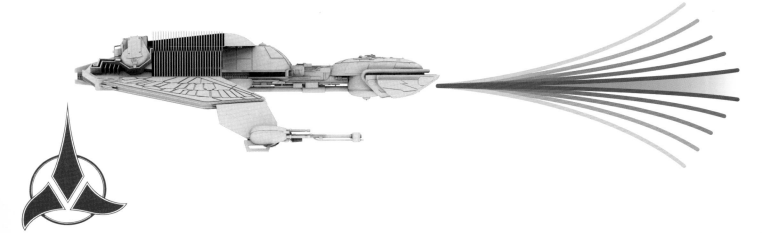

central field flung ahead of the ship by the central deflector—a series of energized plates surrounding the photon torpedo launcher.

The ship's central computer, working with navigational sensor data, deploys the best combination of the different systems to keep the ship safe from interstellar debris in any conditions.

The warp field component generated by the Bird-of-Prey's wings is a general exclusionary field that is naturally created by the warp engine systems. Ionized and non-ionized particles are repelled as long as the ship is at warp. The effective range for deflecting particles by the warp field alone requires a complex formula of particle mass, warp field strength, and relative velocity. To simplify, it is true to say that small particles encountered at low warp would be deflected at a moderately safe distance, while larger particles approaching at high warp would be somewhat more problematic.

The defensive shield grid—a series of energized conduits embedded in the armor and structural layers—adds an additional degree of short-range protection against physical objects at speed by intertwining field lines with the warp emissions and replaces the work done by the warp field at sublight speeds.

The central deflector, which rings the torpedo launcher, uses energy supplied by the ship's plasma conduits, to power multiple layers of field devices. These fields are polarized, acting as a reverse—and one-way—version of a tractor beam or gravity generator, and are effectively repulsor beams. Multiple medium step-down plasma nodes service the central deflector so that if one fails, energy from adjoining conduits can take up the slack. Under computer control, a variety of graviton-related particles and fields can be produced, in waves or in bursts, for scientific or combat purposes.

During flight operations, the full system is usually energized, with the central deflector doing the heavy long-range work. At maximum power output, usually around 125,000MW and supplemented by capacitor banks on Deck 6, particles as large as 2cm can be deflected at velocities up to Warp 8 without steering the deflector field.

While the emitters cannot be physically moved, differential power flows can be used to angle the path of the deflector beam. The focus of the peak radiated power can be moved a total of 5.6 degrees off the centerline in any direction.

This offset effect can move particles up to 3.5cm in size away from the ship.

While the defensive shield grid and armor plating can tolerate occasional micrometeoroid hits at high warp, the interval between armor layer replacements will be shortened. Fortunately, the cross sectional area of the ship and thus the coefficient of interstellar 'drag' is relatively small in comparison to most vessels.

The combat fleets of most other cultures configure their deflectors to extend to at least 15,000,000 kellicams or 30,000,000 kilometers, at a cruising speed of Warp 6, where the fields just begin to push lightly on dust particles. Within one second, shipboard time, those particles are thrust a few thousand meters away. Klingon engineers prefer to cut the distance closer to 10,000,000 kellicams or 20,000,000 kilometers, with a higher power density, giving distant enemy forces less advanced warning during a subspace scan. This means that it takes a few seconds longer to detect a Bird-of-Prey at long range—a tiny advantage, but one the Klingons consider worthwhile.

Although the forward deflector array is not a long-range sensor in the usual sense, the central computer and the navigation subprocessors do reconstruct useable flight and tactical information by measuring the subspace energy that hits the emitter plates. Results from the forward deflector are routinely compared with data coming from numerous other sensors peppering the vessel, including leading-edge wing sensors, combat-sensing devices on the wingtip disruptors, and a trio of front-facing sensors on the hull just aft of the ship's structural neck. Real-time cruise and combat maneuver data derived from the deflector and the other sources is presented on various bridge displays, particularly those of the helm and tactical officers.

▲ The main deflector around the torpedo launcher projects an invisible beam that clears a path in front of the ship.

SHIP'S SYSTEMS

ᴅᴌᴖ ᴊᴇᴜ

Klingon ships may be designed for fighting, but it takes a lot more than disruptors and photon torpedoes to put them in space and keep them there. The ship's support systems may not excite the typical Klingon warrior, but without them a Bird-of-Prey would not be able to leave spacedock let alone enter combat. Without life support the crew would not be able to breathe. Moving around the ship would be almost impossible without the gravity generators that are built into the deck plating. Sensors are essential for plotting the ship's course and detecting her enemies. Communications allow the Bird-of-Prey to receive and give commands and allow the commander to stay in touch with any crew members that have beamed down to a planet surface using the ship's transporters. The landing gear allows it to set down on a planet, while the docking equipment in the nose allows it to connect to other starships and space stations. Without the power of computers the ship would simply drift in space. As with almost everything else on a Bird-of-Prey, the systems are designed with multiple redundancies that ensure that they can still function even after the ship has sustained significant damage. Even the power distribution network is designed to re-route electroplasma around damaged areas to maintain power at all times. And, if everything fails, the ship has a built in autodestruct system that can blow it to pieces, allowing the crew to survive in escape pods ready to fight another day.

The evolution of the modern Bird-of-Prey can be traced back to early vessels that operated only within a planetary atmosphere and were incapable of interstellar flight. Klingon starship builders have never lost sight of that original design and it is a given that every incarnation of the Bird-of-Prey will be able to maneuver in an atmosphere and land on the surface.

Nevertheless setting a starship down on a planet and lifting off again has never been an easy task for the engineers of the Klingon Empire, especially since Klingon impulse engines exhibit more brute force than finesse. 22nd-century Birds-of-Prey, going back as far as one engineering testbed of 2147, relied on an overly large proportion of pure fusion thrust over mass lightening. This meant that the ground crew couldn't get within four kilometers of the ship once the engines were active.

Fortunately, improvements in impulse reaction chambers and driver-coil technology all but eliminated the lethal thermal blast zone and the radius for high-velocity ground debris. Design engineers struggled with ship masses, sizes and masses of landing gear, and propulsion systems until they finally arrived at a combination that worked for routine surface operations.

Operating in a planet's atmosphere proved much less of a challenge than actually supporting the ship once it was on the ground. Since the impulse engines of the day could not lighten the vessel mass as much as the engineers would have liked, the landing pads and their support struts needed to be large and heavy and as a result the earlier Bird-of-Prey required two large open bays to house the folded support struts and landing pads. These bays were so large that the engineers had to cut upward into certain sections of warp engineering in order to accommodate them. Add to the structural parts all of the electrohydraulic conduits, sensor data lines, and plasma power couplings, and Decks 6 and 7 became very cramped spaces.

In the 2280s the landing gear was designed to hold up 236,000 metric tonnes, 110,000 metric tonnes of which is dead weight, at least as far as what the landing legs can 'feel' with the impulse driver coils running at idle. Though the landing gear operates most effectively with the driver coils running, any interruption in impulse power would cause the supports to lock with a local structural integrity field. The struts could support the entire mass, but just barely.

The current *B'rel*-class vessel has smaller support struts and surface pads. While the construction techniques and resulting strength are generally the

▶ The Bird-of-Prey has always been designed to land on a planet's surface, although this presents her designers with some serious challenges.

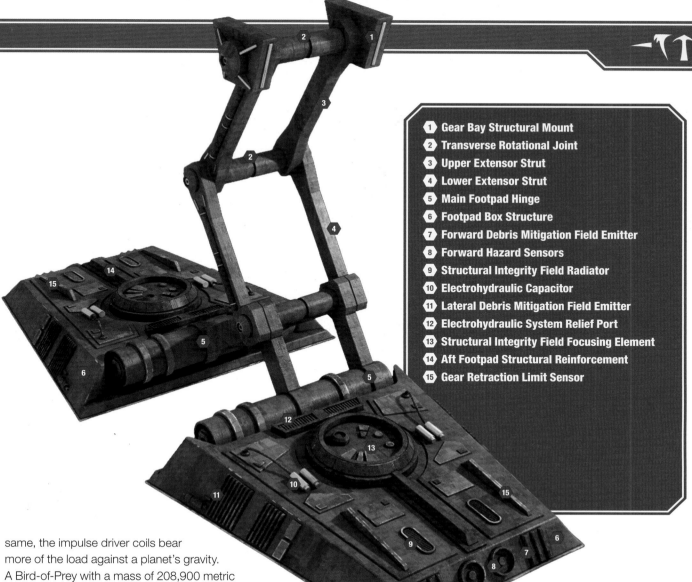

1. Gear Bay Structural Mount
2. Transverse Rotational Joint
3. Upper Extensor Strut
4. Lower Extensor Strut
5. Main Footpad Hinge
6. Footpad Box Structure
7. Forward Debris Mitigation Field Emitter
8. Forward Hazard Sensors
9. Structural Integrity Field Radiator
10. Electrohydraulic Capacitor
11. Lateral Debris Mitigation Field Emitter
12. Electrohydraulic System Relief Port
13. Structural Integrity Field Focusing Element
14. Aft Footpad Structural Reinforcement
15. Gear Retraction Limit Sensor

same, the impulse driver coils bear more of the load against a planet's gravity. A Bird-of-Prey with a mass of 208,900 metric tonnes requires the landing gear to accept only 74,000 metric tonnes of force. This essentially alters the job of the landing pads more to that of placeholders to keep the ship from shifting. As with the previous models, the struts can lock to support the full mass, but even today this is not a recommended operation.

The struts and pads are constructed of multiple layers of common densified tritanium and duranium. The rotating bearings and cylinders are spun from a forced-matrix alloy of berixinite and lorkenium, incredibly strong but almost impossible to machine after cooling, requiring precision fabrication within tolerances the first time.

Landing gear deployment on the *B'rel*-class typically coincides with the change in wing angle to the full-up position. As previously noted, this raises the wingtips and their disruptors above eventual ground level. Planetary approaches and terminal landing sequences can involve many different atmosphere and terrain types, as well as gravity levels. Sensor readings processed by the central computer determine the flight and surface conditions and configure the landing gear and wing hydraulics for approach and touchdown.

The landing gear is useable in environments at or only slightly above Qo'noS-normal gravity with the driver coils at idle. Above an idle setting and into actual impulse hover power, of course, the Bird-of-Prey can manage to make footpad contact with higher gravity worlds. The opposite end of the gravity scale also presents some interesting challenges, including setting down on moons and asteroids. The footpads are equipped with scalable magnetic field coils, used to hold onto nickel-iron or ferrous-analogue bodies in different star systems. In cases of predominantly rocky asteroids, low impulse power can be reversed to press the ship downward. Certain stealth missions or active predator-prey pursuits may require the ship to find a convenient hiding place or observing point.

 **When the *Rotarran* docked at *Deep Space Nine* it did so nose first, hooking up to the station's Cardassian-designed docking ports.**

There are a number of entry hatches around the Bird-of-Prey that can be used to dock with space stations or other vessels. Which and how many hatches are used depends on the type of space structure to which the ship is connecting. Sometimes the ship will dock with small autonomous resupply modules not much bigger than the Bird-of-Prey itself, whereas full orbital shipyards envelop the ship providing multiple connection points. In the case of a space station the Bird-of-Prey will connect nose first using its central docking port, which is installed at the front of Deck 6, inside the pressure cowling surrounding the photon torpedo launcher.

The docking hardware embedded in the Bird-of-Prey's hull and mounted on Decks 5L and 6 includes magnetic grab panels, mooring beam receptors, backup force field emitters, and sensor subsystems. Most of the active equipment is on the yard or space station side, which provides more powerful field emitters and direct yardmaster traffic control. Once the ship has docked, personnel and small cargo can leave the ship through hatches in the pressure cowling.

Docking is a two-step process involving a computer controlled approach and the physical latching up of the vessel to the destination docking port. A safe approach velocity of roughly 5.5 meters per second will get the ship to within 100 meters, by which time the Z-axis of the ship will be almost perfectly aligned with the port on the space station side.

A nominal terminal approach will see the ship slow gradually to 0.3 meters per second prior to force field latchup. In practice, however, especially during wartime, high-speed manual dockings at 2 meters per second have been recorded with commanders relying on their ship's dock force fields and inertial dampeners to cushion the impact.

Under normal conditions, the navigation subroutines used by the Bird-of-Prey typically bring the head end of the ship to within 37 meters of the port before the helm officer releases control of the ship. This is commonly referred to as free-drift mode. The dock mooring beams—essentially narrow focus tractor beams—then engage the vessel, fine tune its rotational attitude and position, and bring it to a full stop in the docked position.

Variations on the sequence occur when the Bird-of-Prey connects with unmanned spacecraft such as the resupply modules. In that case the helm officer retains full control throughout and uses the ship's own field emitters to make the latch-up.

When approaching a non-Klingon station for the first time, sensors and active geometer scanning beams on the ship read the physical construction of the docking port and quickly configure a viable connection, usually in concert with data from the station's computers. Non-Klingon stations that have been previously visited successfully have all docking data pre-processed and stored.

Once the mooring beams and other stabilizing fields are in place, a breathable atmosphere is established between the ship and the transfer tunnel or airlock structure. Most station docks are equipped with annular fields that retain a cylinder of air within the ship-station interface. Computer reminders automatically inform the crew of any pressure or atmospheric composition differences that need to be addressed before hatches are opened on both sides. For the typical Klingon warrior, this is not a problem. Bird-of-Prey crews are trained and medically prepared to adapt to a wide range of ambient conditions, short of those absolutely requiring an environment suit.

While many safety protocols are in place to deal with a dangerous pressure drop in the interface area, most of the docking regulations are more concerned with the structural integrity of the ship while the force fields are at full power. Torsional effects during hostilities, such as weapon hits on a station, can put a strain on the mooring emitters, and crews must be prepared for emergency undockings to head into battle. In the event of an unavoidable undocking, protocols require any crew members who did not make it on board to return via transporter, or if it is not safe drop the shields for transport, the crew members are abandoned and recovered after combat is completed.

In certain rare instances, the opposite of a forced undocking has occurred. Ships have been prevented from undocking as the result of a military situation or factional dispute, and the space station personnel have refused to release the docking clamps and mooring force fields. Deliberately running impulse engines against the pull of mooring beams can have destructive effects on ship and station alike.

Orbital shipyard docks, which accept complete ships into maintenance bays, can extend transfer tunnels to attach to alternate entry hatches, such as the dorsal hatch in the head leading to Deck 4 and the smaller dorsal hatches in the aft hull leading down into the Deck 3 cargo area. Another type of extendable tunnel can attach to the ventral cargo loading ramp at the bottom of Deck 7, though this loading area is more commonly used during planetary landings.

COMMUNICATIONS

Communications aboard a Bird-of-Prey involve a wide variety of familiar devices and technologies, from interdeck voice com to subspace exchanges with the heart of the Empire. Simple but robust optical fiber and RF links connect all decks of the ship to each other and to the bridge, with permanent taps for analyzing and archiving crew orders and actions leading into the central computer.

RF links, along with subspace transceivers, are also built into the handheld crew communicators, data pads, and other portable computing devices. Aboard ship, the interdeck system is the primary system, rather than the personal communicators that are carried by all crew members. Typically 1,289 dedicated voice com channels are hardwired through the Bird-of-Prey using multiple pickups and subprocessor nodes in each pressurized crew area.

During planetside operations, up to a range of 25,000 kellicams or 50,000 kilometers, the crew use personal communicators to communicate with the ship. Larger portable com units have RF segments capable of reaching 400,000 kellicams or 800,000 kilometers, well within an acceptable one-way light time of three seconds.

Some 22 RF transceiver nodes are embedded in the hull layers for external communications, mostly as backup in case subspace communications are degraded. The on-board computer automatically switches between RF com and subspace transmissions,

making the best use of each signal type depending on environmental conditions, electromagnetic interference, and depth below the surface. Scanning instruments using RF and subspace channels will attempt to transmit data instantly, but can also store that data for later transmissions if conditions prevent normal comms channels from operating properly.

On the Bird-of-Prey subspace communications are achieved using a set of six interlinked FTL transceivers built into the subfloor of Deck 5, just aft of the bridge. Each is powered by redundant plasma nodes and backup energy cells. A majority of the subspace com antennae—some 20 out of the 35 built into the structural hull—are located in the head end of the ship. This is done to minimize the lengths of the signal waveguides as well as to keep them clear of possible interference from the warp reactors.

Subspace voice and data transmissions are vital to the coordination of Klingon battle groups and the planning of strategies and tactics during major campaigns. Bird-of-Prey commanders and their communications officers keep in close contact with other ships in their theaters of operation, even when a direct link to the homeworld Qo'noS is not always possible—or desired.

Klingons are extremely security conscious and often very wary of their allies and even other Klingon ships and, as a result, system access and signal encryption codes are frequently changed.

Most deep-space vessels are designed to support environmental conditions approximating the crew's homeworld. Conditions aboard the Bird-of-Prey do not exactly match those at sea level on Qo'noS, but its systems are adequate in terms of maintaining atmospheric composition, temperature, and gravity, limiting radiation levels, providing foodstuffs and liquids, and handling waste. Most engineers in the Empire would argue for exactly that order in terms of which subsystems would receive support and repair attention.

A breathable atmosphere is the first priority. The Bird-of-Prey atmosphere purification and replenishment system consists of 18 small and six large electrostatic processors designed to remove excess carbon dioxide, liberate oxygen molecules, and balance out trace gases from pressurized tanks. The small units are distributed throughout every deck, and the large units are installed three apiece on Decks 4 and 6 in the aft hull. A separate network of 36 circulation pumps move the air around the ship.

Contingency oxygen and nitrogen tanks, integrated with self-powered CO_2 scrubbers, are located on each deck in pressurized compartments that can be sealed off from the central corridors. All processing units are connected to the central computer and plasma power network, and all can operate independently on power cells in the event of a shipboard crisis.

The values in the table below compare conditions at Qo'noS and aboard the Bird-of-Prey

Temperature control, usually in the form of overboard energy dumping, is maintained through a series of liquid ammonia loops. These run through heat exchangers in the hull plating near the wing roots and in the neck. In situations where infrared and other radiation emissions must be kept at a minimum, as in stealth operations, all heat-producing hardware is dropped to minimum power and excess energy is stored temporarily in special chambers in the impulse engine section. In situations where warp core loss could lead to vessel cooling, the Bird-of-Prey is well insulated and can keep a working temperature of 16°C using a single fusion generator at low output, and through localized emergency heaters for up to 420 days.

The crew are protected against ionizing radiation by a combination of external hull shielding, internal bulkheads, and medical anti-radiation treatment. Various shipboard systems as well as enemy weapons fire can produce radiation, resulting in everything from long-term genetic damage to burns, organ failure and death if not treated quickly. The typical regimens include hypospray injections of apchelicine and programmable implants dispensing odulenine, both effective in countering tissue breakdown. As a point of reference, the normal background radiation on Qo'noS is measured at 3.2 milliWd per year, compared to the exposure on a ship assignment of 41.6 milliWd per year, easily countered by the medical officer. The baseline 1Wd indicates death within one year if not treated.

Food and liquid storage on a Bird-of-Prey is basically a one-way or 'open' system. A typical mission profile makes cargo accommodations for enough live and processed animal products for 36 warriors for a 33-day duty cycle. This amounts to some 2,300 kilograms normally consumed, with an added margin of 600 kilograms for extended time away from a resupply vessel or shipyard. This total of 2,900 kilograms does not include any live targs brought aboard.

While Klingon nutritional scientists factor all potable liquids into their life-support calculations, they know full well that the beverage of choice is Klingon bloodwine, chosen by the commander and presented to his—or her—crew as symbolic payment for their services and loyalty. The usual load transferred to a departing Bird-of-Prey can be as many as 30 barrels to last the entire mission. Bottles of various other Klingon drinks are usually found in the ship's stores or the commander's cabin, including *Mot'loch*, *Bahgol*, *Chech'tluh*, and *Warnog*. In addition to the above, 300 gallons of *Raktajino* are typically consumed during a single mission, when warriors need to stay sharply focused.

The recycling of foodstuffs and both potable liquids and water for various shipboard purposes has almost never been been practiced on the *B'rel*-class, though the equipment does exist on Decks 5 and 6 in the event it becomes necessary to do so. Most ships in distress have been recovered before a quarter of their emergency rations, normally 320 small daily containers, run out. Simulations indicate that ships adrift with minimal power can supply their crews with recycled nutrients for another 380 days beyond the end of the rations.

QO'NOS		BIRD-OF-PREY	
Nitrogen	77.20%	Nitrogen	78.11%
Oxygen	19.60%	Oxygen	18.80%
Neon	1.70%	Neon	1.90%
Xenon	1.41%	Xenon	1.01%
Carbon Dioxide	0.05%	Carbon Dioxide	0.08%
Trace Gases	0.04%	Trace Gases	0.10%

Gravity aboard a Bird-of-Prey is produced by a network of overlapping field generators that are built into the floor of every deck. The generators, which are installed both singly and in groups of six, are energized by small power taps from the EPS (electroplasma) conduits that run throughout the ship.

The majority of generators are mounted inside the deck floor, which has a hollow structure with an average height of 43.6cm. The standard generator measures 29.14cm in diameter and is 10.52cm tall. The combined groups of six generators, which include a central controller hub, span 90.37cm. The generators are attached to the deck base plates or gratings, facing upward. Servicing or replacement can be done through local decking access hatches. Additional generators are fitted to the walls of the ship to create a correctly balanced gravity field.

The generators work by exposing a small liquid-grown sphere of crystal direkkasine fluorite—typically 2.33cm in diameter—to high-frequency plasma pulses. The crystal lattice structure alters the incoming plasma, breaking the streams into millions of discrete subatomic packets and creating a spray of gravitons, elementary particles that create gravity. These are dispersed in all directions radiating from each generator, and create a gravity field that pulls everything the gravitons touch back towards their source. Because the gravitons are not polarized as in Starfleet vessels, each generator is backed by a carbonitrium shield disk that absorbs downward firing gravitons and effectively drops them into subspace. This prevents the gravity field in one deck from pulling objects and personnel to the ceiling of the deck below.

A superconducting ring is built into the generator disk to keep the graviton emitter running for up to 3.5 hours in the event of a plasma shutdown, decreasing the perceived gravity slowly over the final few minutes. However, it is not unheard of for ships to lose gravity if the EPS system is overloaded.

The strength of gravity on board the ship is controlled by the ship's lower computer core, which can address individual generators as well as the group hubs. The Qo'noS normal surface acceleration is equivalent to 1.2g Earth gravity, but Klingons often make adjustments to the gravity in localised areas of the ship. Lighter gravity can be helpful in moving certain cargo loads, assisting injured warriors in the medical bay, and in making some types of repairs in the engineering spaces. Heavier gravity, while also helpful with engineering problems, is mainly used during warrior combat training.

1 **Graviton Emitter Crystal**
2 **Graviton Diffusion Arrays**
3 **Carbonitrium Blocking Disk**
4 **Superconducting Power Backup**
5 **Generator Support Strut**
6 **Generator Cluster Controller Hub**

▼ **Gravity on board a Bird-of-Prey is created by a series of graviton emitters built into the deck plating.**

L ike all other interstellar space vessels the Bird-of-Prey relies heavily on computerized systems to manage every aspect of ship operations, including propulsion, navigation, weapons systems, transporter functions, environmental control, and communications.

The Bird-of-Prey has a single central computer core that consists of two highly redundant cylindrical processor module decks and a lower section designed primarily for rapid mass data storage and retrieval.

The stack is a substantial module that is more than 6m tall and reaches from the top of Deck 5L to the bottom of Deck 6. Bands of sensors, identical to those surrounding Deck 5, ring the hull just outside the core and specialized instruments make up the bulk of the lower sensor cap.

Both processor decks are 11.42m in diameter and 2.3m in height. The storage and retrieval deck is also 11.42m across but slightly shorter at 1.56m.

All the core framing structures are fabricated from densified duranium foam bonded with hafnium titanide and include integral power and data channels. Connections to the plasma power nodes and the ship's systems can be made quickly during installation. During repair yard layovers the entire core can be swapped out robotically in less than two hours.

▼ **Like almost all advanced species, Klingons use isolinear circuitry to store data.**

The crew access the outer hatches of all three sections of the stack using a set of circular catwalks and ladders that were moved into place after the core was installed. Access to the open center of the stack for maintenance tasks is made through a pressure hatch in the floor of Deck 5, just aft of the bridge. The open well also leads down to an equipment and torpedo transport tunnel that can provide emergency exit from the ship through the torpedo launcher cowling on Deck 6.

Isolinear memory and processing technology is widespread across the Alpha and Beta Quadrants of the Galaxy, though it is implemented differently by different races. Klingon use of isolinear circuits is distinguished by a marked difference in the sizes and densities of the crystal cells manufactured for space vessels and those used in most every other sector of Klingon society.

Advanced isolinear research on Qo'noS has yielded some of the smallest crystal cells ever seen, almost too small to hold information reliably at ~9nm, but the stability is reinforced by a pulsed subspace field that imparts no changes to the data. However, the ruggedized isolinear chips installed in the Bird-of-Prey's computer cores have relatively large crystal cells at 23nm and measure 10.8cm x 5.8cm x 0.9cm. Each chip can hold approximately 62.7 kiloquads of data. The total quantities of chips, protective racks, and data connections can vary widely depending on the individual Bird-of-Prey and its key missions, but the complete base computer core accommodates upwards of 15,000 chips, equalling a capacity of some 940,000 kiloquads.

The circuit pathways impressed on the isolinear slabs and the organization of the plug-in racks closely mimic Klingon cortical cells and larger brain structures. The interconnections within the core are designed to be as short as possible, using a combination of nanopulse optical fiber as well as a conductive carbon ribbon as a backup pathway. Signal switching nodes, mounted inboard of the chip racks, perform all of the AI data routing tasks within the core as well as handling all incoming sensor inputs and shipboard systems upkeep.

The computer core is linked to all ship systems, including remote terminals, by additional bundles of optical fiber and carbon ribbon, with RF connectivity as a backup. The total length of physical fiber on the ship is nearly 2,500km.

The lower processor deck typically takes on the management of the majority of basic ship systems while the upper deck, closer to the bridge, is primarily concerned with combat maneuvers and weapons. Both decks interact, comparing readings and making decisions on flight operations, power allocations, communications, and other mission parameters, and both decks record and extract data from the lower storage section.

In the event of a catastrophic failure within the core, usually from battle, artificial intelligence routines will automatically determine the severity of the damage and reconfigure all healthy processors to prioritize tasks, according to the ship's situation and in concert with commands from the bridge crew.

Damaged isolinear elements and switching nodes can be swapped out as opportunities allow, and the core can work around the remaining damaged circuits.

The Bird-of-Prey can typically function with as little as 15 per cent of the computer 'awake' and transfer

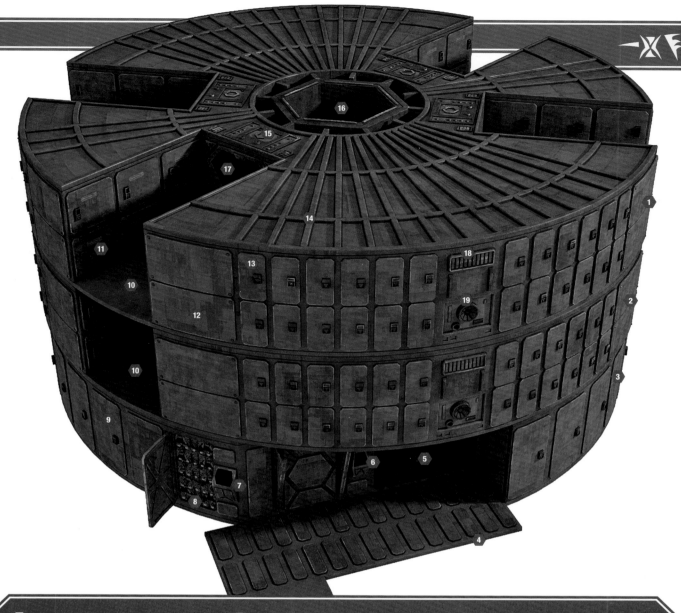

Key

1. Upper Processor Module
2. Lower Processor Module
3. Data Storage & Retrieval Module
4. Torpedo & Equipment Transfer Track
5. Torpedo & Equipment Transfer Tunnel
6. Transfer Tunnel Control Console
7. Data Storage Inventory Control
8. Isolinear Chip Racks (1400)
9. Isolinear Storage Access Hatch (24)
10. Processor Module Monitor Alcove (8)
11. Special-Purpose Processor Racks (96)
12. Outer Processor Rack Storage (32)
13. Processor Rack Storage (104)
14. Duranium Titanide Framing
15. Power & Data Channel Connectors (24)
16. Deck 5 Core Access Well
17. Processor Systems Monitor Panel (8)
18. Computer Core Cooling Duct (4)
19. Optical Fiber Connector (4)

authority to major systems such as the warp and impulse engines, whose smaller dedicated computer modules are capable of executing basic flight commands from the bridge.

A functioning Bird-of-Prey with at least 45 per cent overall computer capacity can, in an after-battle scenario, fly in formation with a more damaged vessel, taking over many of the latter's functions via a subspace connection.

As with most Klingon spacecraft, the Bird-of-Prey has been designed to operate for at least a century with little change in the basic configuration. In the hundred years or so that the current design of Bird-of-Prey has been in service, internal systems including the computer core have undergone periodic, though still limited, upgrades. This allows Klingon shipyards to build vessels at a rapid rate when needed and ensures that standard spares will fit and function.

▲ The main computer core consists of three decks that run from Deck 5 to the area beneath Deck 6 in the head of the Bird-of-Prey.

Matter transporters have been a standard part of Klingon space vessels for at least the last two centuries. Constant improvements in transporter subsystems have been made across the fleet, while preserving the basic hardware standards for energy connections, phase transition coils, pattern buffers, and computer controls. The Bird-of-Prey makes efficient use of large transporter assemblies on Decks 4 and 5 linked together in the aft hull as well as smaller units located forward in the head structure. The shipboard system can transport personnel and cargo at high resolution up to 49,000 kilometers or some 24,500 kellicams using line-of-sight targeting through vacuum or atmosphere. Beaming through unshielded solid objects can be accomplished only if the material thickness in meters, divided by the density in grams per cubic centimeter, is less than 200. This factor allows for transport through roughly a kilometer of planetary rock and, by contrast, a few meters of refined metals and composites. This still results in an appreciable capability to move warriors and their gear in a wide range of scenarios.

The largest transporter pads on the *B'rel*-class are on Deck 4 just forward of the main cargo bay, in a pair of compartments off the central transfer aisle. Each pad can accommodate six warriors or a mixed grouping of warriors and cargo containers or weapons lockers. Directly below on Deck 5 is a smaller transporter room with a pad sized to take two warriors. The final two pads, each sized for a single warrior, are forward on Deck 5, accessible from the main corridor just behind the bridge. Each cargo pad is connected to its own major plasma power conduit, toroidal pattern buffer, and optional biofilter, all submerged into the decking. Built into the decking above are the combined energizing and phase transition coils, and molecular imaging scanner. The hardware at both ends of Deck 5 is set up in a similar manner, and all transporter operations are controlled by segments of the central computer. Fifteen transport emitter arrays, which send and receive the actual matter streams, are embedded in the hull plating just below the outermost *kar'dasnoth* armor layer. Target scanning by the ship's sensors determines which emitters will hold the best lock for beaming.

Once the relative motions of the ship and target are known, the computer will decide if the system is ready and operating properly. The molecular imaging scanner builds a real time, though temporary, record of the pattern of the warrior or cargo being dematerialized for transport. The phase transition coils, working like millions of tiny quantum manipulators, perform the matter disassembly on the subatomic scale and send an unbroken stream to the pattern buffer. The magnetically shielded buffer torus is able to hold the contents of a pad without pattern degradation for up to four minutes, regardless of transport direction. Various options exist for sending a pattern on to its destination, or aborting and rematerializing. After four minutes the spiral field winding around the matter stream will begin to uncouple and the pattern could be lost.

Klingon transporters utilize a clustered set of seven confinement beams to keep the matter stream intact, one central beam surrounding the stream and six 'empty' beams protecting the center, all traversing space and low density matter with a cross section of 3.2 centimeters. Once the stream begins to exit the emitter, there is no recalling it, and all hardware must be operating at peak performance levels. Streams that are recovered in a true transporter chamber have a better chance of rematerialization than those happening elsewhere on a ship or on a planetary surface, but the technology is reliable enough today that most cultures are not concerned with possible accidents. In combat, however, transporters can be damaged, patterns can be dispersed by weapons fire, and warriors can be lost. As with the escape pods, strict protocols are in place governing the use of transporters to leave a ship in battle. After all other options are exhausted, a working transporter can be used to save warriors to fight again and to protect vital wartime intelligence.

The network of charged conduits running through the Bird-of-Prey consists of three branching systems, all fed by the ship's three energy sources. The primary—and most energetic—system begins with the twin warp cores in Main Engineering. By itself, the warp plasma produced from matter and antimatter could power all the ship's other systems combined for at least ten years, and for general ground-based power generation this scheme has been used quite efficiently. Driving the ship at high warp, however, consumes some 95 per cent of the reactor output. The remaining 5 per cent is enough to power the other systems required during warp flight.

The impulse fusion reactors, the next tier down, can also power all of the ship's basic systems without factoring in propulsion. The third level, stored energy power cells, are mostly used in last-resort emergencies to operate life support and communications.

Depending on the situation, all power systems can be linked for maximum interoperability and have been deliberately designed for battle conditions where one or more sources will be running in a degraded condition.

Even in normal operating modes, the energy distribution system still features a high level of built-in redundancy. The six major taps from the large transverse warp core conduit connect to twelve high-power step-down nodes. These nodes reduce the volume, pressure, and temperature of the plasma to levels useable by the photon torpedo launcher, shields, navigational deflector, cloak generator, and transporters.

The plasma conduits branching off from the step-down nodes are generally 25–35cm in size, either round or rectangular in cross section and are routed through the decking. The conduits are typically constructed of duranium with a 0.5cm *baakten* lining and a woven carbonitrium outer layer for insulation. Magnetic gate valves control both the input and output of the nodes, and are constantly monitored and balanced by the central computer core.

Four of the nodes are located in Main Engineering, two near each core. One node is installed near the center of Deck 6 in the aft hull, four at the interface with the ship's neck, two at the back of Deck 5 behind the bridge, and one off-center on Deck 6 near the torpedo launcher.

Thirty medium taps off the transverse conduit connect to an equal number of medium-power step-down nodes. This provides conduit branches that are around 11cm in diameter. At this scale, the EM charge carried in the pressurized gas is still 'hot' enough to power the electromechanical wing actuators, active sensors, life support, central computer, and subspace communications. Each medium step-down node contains three connectors, making a possible total of 90 branches, though only 60 are normally active. The remaining 30 connectors are used for emergency rerouting via flex conduits.

Five of the 11cm conduits connect to the smallest step-down nodes, which are designed for shipboard devices and services. These systems include weapon and communicator recharge stations, lighting, intra-ship communications, pressure doors, and cargo lifts. Some 650 power cables—hollow conduits that are 1–3cm across—fan out to various compartments from bundles and junctions within the decking.

Emergency power cells are grouped throughout the ship, each containing a computer subnode able to maintain a data network on energy allocation if the warp and impulse reactors fail. The total emergency power system includes a pair of deuterium microfusion reactors, similar to the thrust units on a photon torpedo but self contained and measuring 49cm in diameter. The total runtime on one of these small units is 13 days based on a single insulated fuel canister.

The sensor systems on the *B'rel*-class prioritize short-range operation and are optimized for combat. The long-range sensors, which are principally used in plotting a course, are far less developed. To the Klingon mind, the sensor systems and data subprocessors used in distant warp travel are only considered helpful in two instances: getting to a battle and going home victorious. Everything in between is made possible by dedicated instruments mounted on and in the hull plating, plus multiple bands of protected sensors peering out into space.

The long-range sensors involve basic instruments for navigation and space hazard avoidance at both warp and impulse speeds,

but also include a small number of devices tuned to search out spacecraft structural materials and engine emissions. Most commanders need only a general indication that a target is out in the far distance, matches a vessel in the computer database, and is maneuvering in a particular way. Closer inspection with the short-range sensors usually confirms a commander's suspicions. The long-range sensor group includes:

- Galactic EM Doppler Detector
- Stellar Position Comparator
- Subatomic Spectral Analyzer
- Ion Trail Detector
- Subspace Waveform Imager

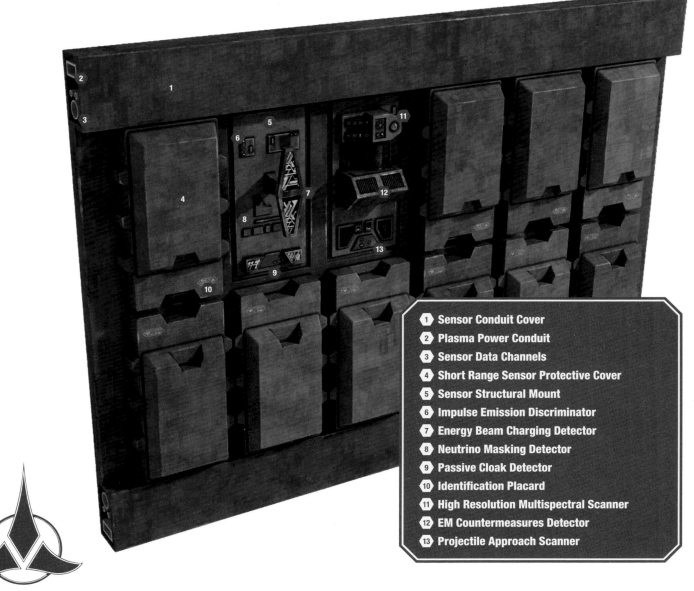

1. Sensor Conduit Cover
2. Plasma Power Conduit
3. Sensor Data Channels
4. Short Range Sensor Protective Cover
5. Sensor Structural Mount
6. Impulse Emission Discriminator
7. Energy Beam Charging Detector
8. Neutrino Masking Detector
9. Passive Cloak Detector
10. Identification Placard
11. High Resolution Multispectral Scanner
12. EM Countermeasures Detector
13. Projectile Approach Scanner

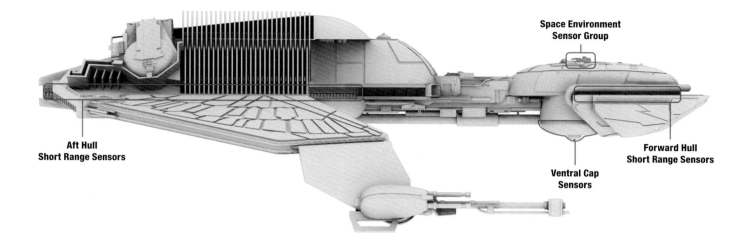

**Aft Hull
Short Range Sensors**

**Space Environment
Sensor Group**

**Ventral Cap
Sensors**

**Forward Hull
Short Range Sensors**

The navigation and targeting routines in the central computer use the readings from these sensors, plus any incoming EM radiation data from the forward deflector, to synthesize a view of the surrounding space to a radius of two light-years with medium resolution, and out to three light-years with slightly lower resolution. If Klingon or allied vessels are within these spheres, cleaner data may be exchanged by subspace and integrated into the overall view. Tactical programs in the computer constantly analyze incoming long-range data, reporting on conditions related to the current mission, or prioritizing targets of opportunity.

The short-range sensors ring the outside of the vessel in two major bands. The largest set covers the aft hull, surrounding Deck 5 with upper and lower rows, extending all the way to the space between the two impulse engine groups. The smaller set encompasses the central computer, and a special set of conformal EM instruments cover the computer's lower hull cap.

The majority of the instruments are designed for combat applications, with some devoted more to planetary and star system data collection. The computer sensor ring possesses some of the shortest data waveguides on the ship, delivering real-time data at a speed where nanoseconds could mean the difference between hitting a target and becoming one.

The ventral cap sensors are tuned to see the wingtip disruptors, especially with the wings in the dropped attack position, and can track their intended targets. They also see the photon torpedo firing trajectories, processing relative target velocities

and positions 460 times per second for up to 200 individual moving vessels.

The aft hull sensor bands add to the complete battle-environment picture, and are helpful in identifying pursuing attackers. All short-range sensors are equipped with fast vessel identification circuits, necessary in battles involving criss-crossing combatants in order to prevent accidental friendly hits.

Tactical software reading the incoming data focus on target ranges, attitudes, and flight vectors, bringing sophisticated predictive motion routines into play. This renders any unconventional enemy maneuvering nearly useless at sublight speeds. The typical short-range sensor group includes:

- **High Resolution Multispectral Scanner**
- **Impulse Emission Discriminator**
- **Hull Deformation Scanner**
- **Passive Cloak Detector**
- **Low-level Thermal Imager**
- **Neutrino Masking Detector**
- **Projectile Approach Scanner**
- **Energy Beam Charging Detector**
- **EM Countermeasures Detector**

The ship mounted sensors can be supplemented by data collected by instrument probes, which are useful in both intelligence-gathering missions and planetary resource searches. The probes are equipped with sensors derived from those on the hull and fitted to modified photon-torpedo casings. As with the antimatter mines, intelligence probes can loiter for many months in passive mode and then perform their mission.

MAINTENANCE SCHEDULE

SYSTEM	COMPONENT	REPLACE EVERY
DISRUPTOR CANNONS	PRIMARY CANNON EMITTER SECONDARY CANNONS SECOND-STAGE ACCELERATOR	18,000 SHOTS 16,000 SHOTS 4,500 SHOTS
TORPEDO LAUNCHER	LAUNCH TUBE PLASMA POWER CONNECTOR	3,750 SHOTS 2,800 SHOTS
CLOAKING GENERATOR	WARP CORE PLASMA TAP TELEPORT WAVEFORM ACCELERATOR CLOAKING FIELD EMITTER	1390 CYCLES 560 CYCLES 2700 CYCLES
DEFENSIVE SHIELDS	SHIELD WAVEGUIDE LAYER SHIELD GENERATOR FIELD AMPLIFIERS	AS NECESSARY* 3 YEARS 4.7 YEARS
WARP ENGINES	UPPER/LOWER REACTOR CORE SHOCK ABSORBERS ANTIMATTER MANIFOLD TRANSVERSE PLASMA CONDUIT DEUTERIUM INJECTOR ANTIMATTER INJECTOR	15.6 YEARS 6.8 YEARS 4.9 YEARS 11.1 YEARS 3.3 YEARS 4.9 YEARS
ANTIMATTER STORAGE	ANTIMATTER POD MAGNETIC LINER MAGNETIC CONDUIT NETWORK	4.9 YEARS 4.9 YEARS
DILITHIUM	DILITHIUM CRYSTALS CONTROLLER HOUSING	3900 HOURS 9.3 YEARS
WARP WING	WARP SYSTEM PRESSURE VESSEL PLASMA MANIFOLD WARP PLASMA INJECTORS PLASMA VENTING COOLANT PROPULSION SYSTEMS CAPACITORS	22 YEARS 9.8 YEARS 5.2 YEARS 2.6 YEARS 5.8 YEARS
IMPULSE SYSTEM	VECTORED EXHAUST DIRECTOR FUSION REACTOR SPACE-TIME DRIVER COILS WARP PLASMA CONDUIT	6.7 YEARS 9.2 YEARS 12.3 YEARS 9.8 YEARS
RCS THRUSTERS	ENTIRE THRUSTER ASSEMBLY	6.5 YEARS
NAVIGATIONAL DEFLECTOR	DEFLECTOR FIELD GENERATORS	22.3 YEARS
LANDING GEAR	TRANSVERSE ROTATIONAL JOINTS MAIN FOOTPAD HINGE STRUCTURAL INTEGRITY FIELD UNIT	650 LANDINGS 650 LANDINGS 1500 LANDINGS
DOCKING SYSTEM	MOORING BEAM RECEPTORS ATMOSPHERE FIELD CONTAINMENT	2500 CYCLES 1300 CYCLES
ENERGY DISTRIBUTION	PLASMA POWER CONDUITS STEP-DOWN NODES	11.1 YEARS 5.2 YEARS
GRAVITY GENERATORS	ENTIRE GENERATOR ASSEMBLY CONTROLLER HUB	5.4 YEARS 5.4 YEARS
COMMUNICATION SYSTEMS	RF RECEIVER NODES SUBSPACE TRANSCEIVERS	22.3 YEARS 5.7 YEARS
SENSORS	SENSOR COVERS SENSOR INTERNALS	15.5 YEARS 3.2 YEARS
MAIN COMPUTER	ISOLINEAR CHIP RACKS SPECIAL-PURPOSE PROCESSORS OPTICAL FIBER BUNDLES	1.5 YEARS 2.3 YEARS 5.6 YEARS
TRANSPORTER SYSTEMS	PHASE TRANSITION COILS PATTERN BUFFER TORUS	680 CYCLES 740 CYCLES
LIFE SUPPORT SYSTEM	ELECTROSTATIC PROCESSORS CIRCULATION PUMPS AMMONIA TEMPERATURE LOOPS	12,600 HOURS 11,400 HOURS 9,600 HOURS
AUTO-DESTRUCT SYSTEM	ENTIRE DESTRUCT PACKAGE	2.2 YEARS
ESCAPE PODS	ENTIRE POD, SYSTEM CHECKOUT	5.4 YEARS
CONTROL CONSOLES	INTERNAL DISPLAY UNIT COMPUTER SUBNODE	AS NECESSARY AS NECESSARY

*COMBAT HULL DAMAGE REPAIRS

Whenever a situation arises requiring the total deliberate destruction of a Bird-of-Prey, a series of internal explosive packages can be detonated. These are designed to rupture the anitmatter pods and cause a catastrophic explosion.

There are six such packages in the autodestruct system, distributed among the antimatter pod racks in Main Engineering. Klingon ship designers as far back as 2137 have included ordinance powerful enough and fast enough to rupture all standard pods simultaneously, which on the *B'rel*-class number 20. The resulting instantaneous loss of magnetic containment produces an explosion that not only blows the vessel apart but consumes the expanding cloud of alloys and composites in a blinding matter-antimatter reaction.

The explosive package itself is relatively unsophisticated in its construction and operation, and highly effective within the short range it needs to work. The duranium housing, a flattened diamond shape measuring 1.21m wide, 0.78m high, and 2.43m in length, is sized to fit the rack space between the upper and lower rows of antimatter pods. The package contains four hardened conical penetrators backed by a shaped explosive charge. The penetrator is a multilayered projectile built up from forced molecular matrices of tungsten, kratysite, and hafnium.

In contrast to the basic physical specifications, the safety interlocks and detonator programming are far more complex. In order to ensure that all six packages receive the activation pulse at precisely

the same time, the electroplasma power conduits and data cables are exactly the same length, and test pulses are measured and adjusted for any power flow discrepancies or data lag. There is no direct radio frequency trigger, though destruct signals from outside the ship can be authenticated through protected nodes of the central computer.

Command authority codes to set the autodestruct in motion normally come from the commander and first officer, or lower-level officers only if no verified life signs can be detected by the computer either on board the ship or in escape pods. Countdown timing can be set in escape scenarios to allow for a survivable blast radius. Tables of hundreds of destruct conditions have been simulated and programmed in the central computer and the package subprocessors. Most deal with preventing enemy forces from taking the ship or extracting classified data in battle.

▲ The ship can be destroyed by detonating a series of charges in the antimatter storage racks. They release the antimatter in the pods causing a massive explosion.

1. Duranium Housing
2. Anti-Tamper Signal Shields
3. Housing Service Locks
4. Passive Cooling System Radiator
5. Status Indicator
6. Power Level Indicator
7. Conical Penetrator

ᕈᕈᕦᗌᗇᖉᕋ ᖉᕦᕦᕓᕦᕃᕃ ESCAPE PODS

Contrary to popular belief, Birds-of-Prey are routinely fitted with escape pods. The Klingons' willingness to die in battle should not be confused with a death wish. In the words of Kahless, it is better to win a war than to lose a battle gloriously. This is not to say that Klingons use escape pods lightly. In fact, a Bird-of-Prey is equipped with only enough escape pods for 24 people—two-thirds of a standard crew—and there are strict conventions governing their use.

In combat, the ship must already have sustained heavy casualties and there must be no realistic prospect of the ship itself surviving. In the classic scenario envisaged by the Klingon Defense Force, at least ten crewmembers will have been lost and the ship must be in imminent danger of being destroyed or boarded. In this situation, the ideal tactic is to program the computers to ram the nearest enemy vessel while the surviving crewmembers use the escape pods.

The intention behind using the escape pods is for warriors to survive to fight again, not to be taken prisoner, so in order to prevent the pods being retrieved by the enemy, they are fitted with a small matter-antimatter charge that can be activated by the pod's users if it is tractored or beamed into an enemy ship. The resulting explosion has a far lower yield than a photon torpedo, but is sufficient to severely damage a ship. If the

occupants are beamed straight out of the escape pod, their primary duty is to return to the fight so they will allow themselves to be taken prisoner. Suicide is not considered an honorable option as long as there are enemies still to fight or hope of escape.

If the Bird-of-Prey is not in combat and has suffered a catastrophic systems failure such as a warp-core breach, a serious radiation leak or a life-support failure, then it is acceptable for everyone except the engineering staff to use the escape pods. The engineers are expected to stay on board until the last moment, doing everything possible to save their ship. The Klingons reason that a serious malfunction must be the engineers' fault. If they can remedy it then they deserve to live; if they cannot, it is right for them to die. No engineer who allowed his ship to suffer such a serious malfunction that it was destroyed would ever be allowed to serve on a Klingon ship again, and most Klingon engineers would rather die than suffer the humiliation of abandoning a malfunctioning ship.

The pods themselves are designed to accommodate two people, and can provide life support for a total of 18 days for two or 36 days for one. They are fitted with a small impulse engine that uses a fusion reaction to propel the escape pod away from the ship. The engine has enough fuel to fire a second time to send the pod into the atmosphere of a nearby planet. The shielding

▼ Although it is not something they talk about much, Klingon ships are fitted with escape pods that ensure their warriors live to fight another day.

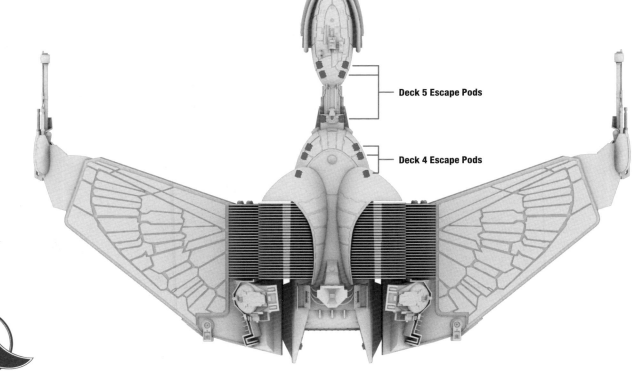

Deck 5 Escape Pods

Deck 4 Escape Pods

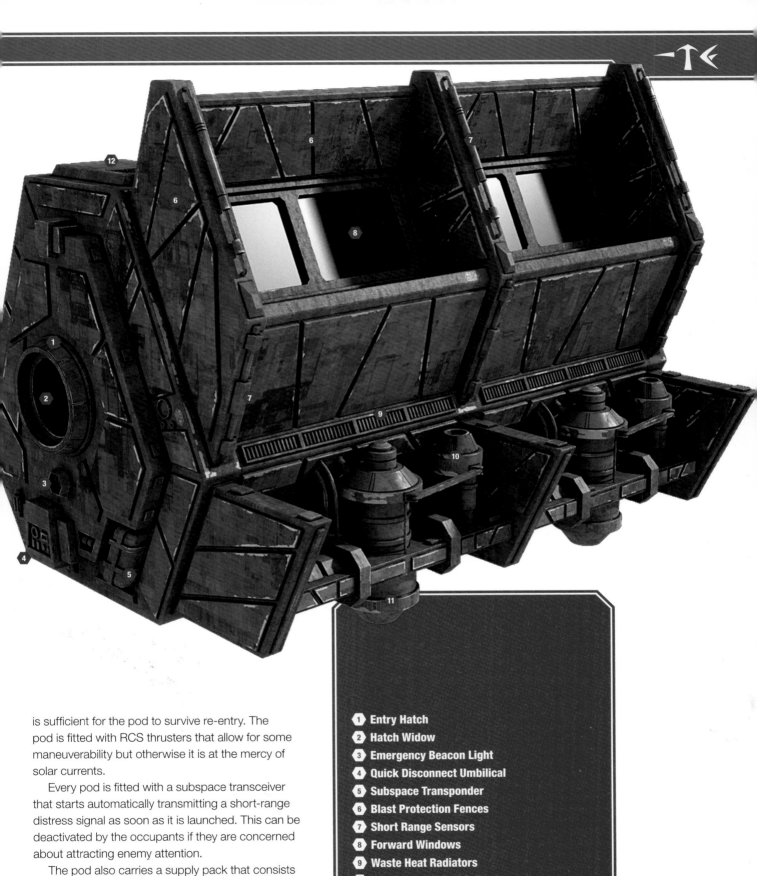

is sufficient for the pod to survive re-entry. The pod is fitted with RCS thrusters that allow for some maneuverability but otherwise it is at the mercy of solar currents.

Every pod is fitted with a subspace transceiver that starts automatically transmitting a short-range distress signal as soon as it is launched. This can be deactivated by the occupants if they are concerned about attracting enemy attention.

The pod also carries a supply pack that consists of emergency rations, a hand disruptor and a *d'k tahg*. The subspace transmitter can be removed and turned into a portable unit and the thrusters can be converted into heaters.

1. Entry Hatch
2. Hatch Widow
3. Emergency Beacon Light
4. Quick Disconnect Umbilical
5. Subspace Transponder
6. Blast Protection Fences
7. Short Range Sensors
8. Forward Windows
9. Waste Heat Radiators
10. Emergency Shield Subsystem
11. Microfusion Power Reactor
12. Dorsal Attitude Control System

LIFE ON BOARD

ᴅ◁ᒥ ◡ᴡℲ

There are few places a Klingon warrior would rather be than serving on a Bird-of-Prey and life on board ship reflects all the famous Klingon virtues. As every Klingon will tell you, "a Klingon is his work" so the accommodation is spartan with little room for personal possessions. The only concessions to leisure are training halls where warriors can practice martial arts and weapons drills and a mess hall where the crew consume live food and bloodwine. The vast majority of their time is spent either operating the ship or preparing for battle.

Life on board ship also reflects the complex realities of Klingon society, with the officers acting as a ruling class, who are followed by warriors and servants. But, like everything in Klingon life, this strict social hierarchy is earned with the crew members literally fighting for their place in the pecking order and commanders only maintaining their position by avoiding assassination.

There is no question that it is a hard life, but it is one that Klingon warriors dream of. On a well-run ship under a good captain like Martok, the ship provides a perfect microcosm without any of the complications of society at large. Every man and woman knows his place, virtue is rewarded, cowardice is punished and honor and victory await everyone.

Life on board a Klingon ship is famously full-blooded. Discipline is fierce and no species works harder than the Klingons. They drill themselves almost constantly, practice hand-to-hand combat in their 'leisure' time, and devote themselves to studying their enemies and considering new tactics. But life on a successful Bird-of-Prey is also joyous. When a crew is happy the bridge rings out with the sound of opera as officers sing while they work. In the mess hall, mighty warriors hold court telling tales of their great deeds and laughing with one another. Victories are celebrated with bloodwine and more song. There is no place a Klingon warrior would rather be than on a Bird-of-Prey heading into battle.

To outsiders life on a Klingon ship sounds brutal, brawling is common with warriors stiking each other to impose discipline and fighting to establish dominance. Each member of the crew may challenge his superior and even kill him. However, life on board ship is strictly hierarchical: a crew member may only strike his subordinates and injuries are rarely serious (though the Klingon definition of minor injuries includes broken bones). If a crew member strikes an equal or a superior, this will commonly result in a challenge to the death. But far from being chaotic, these challenges are one of the key methods used to maintain discipline on board ship.

Officers are prevented from abusing their power because each crewman literally has the duty to challenge his superior if he sees any signs of weakness, cowardice, failure to perform their duty or dishonorable behavior. Each member of the crew can only challenge his direct superior and there are strict rules for how a challenge can be made and under what circumstances. If a challenge is successful and the crew member kills his superior, he takes his place and advances in rank, but challenges are not undertaken lightly. If a warrior succeeds in killing his former superior, but does not have the support of the crew, it is inevitable that he himself will be challenged and this would almost certainly lead to his death.

There are also limits to how far a Klingon can advance by challenging his superior. A servant cannot become a warrior as the result of a challenge, and a warrior cannot become an officer.

Klingon society is dominated by the Great Houses, which have something close to a monopoly on the training of officers. However, one of the great strengths of the Klingon Empire is its willingness to promote men through the ranks. No less a person than Chancellor

Martok started his career as a servant before being given a battlefield commission and rising through the ranks to become a captain, then a general, supreme commander of the Ninth Fleet, and then eventually Chancellor.

It remains true that this kind of promotion only happens on a large scale in wartime when a warrior can distinguish himself, and access to the officers' academy is still largely restricted to the nobility. It has been argued that Klingon society is structurally unsuitable for peace and becomes corrupted if good men don't have the opportunity to advance. Many Klingon historians regard K'mpec's long peace (2348–2367) as a disastrous period that led to the corruption of the upper echelons of society, because relatively few men were promoted through the ranks.

In fact, when a Klingon is assigned to a Bird-of-Prey he or she fervently hopes that their posting will lead to an honorable death in the service of the Empire. It is a commonplace in Klingon society that 'there are no old warriors' and Klingons who are unfortunate to survive into old age are regarded with equal measures of scorn and pity. As a consequence the ship's crew is almost always young and vigorous. There are some exceptions and particularly honored old warriors are able to find service on a Bird-of-Prey, but they are far from common. Although Klingon warriors aspire to a death in combat, they have no desire for an unnecessary demise and are often wary of older commanders who may have something of a deathwish.

That vigor often finds an outlet in leisure time, when the crew drink heavily, sing and joke with one another. Since crews consist of both men and women, it is not uncommon for crew members to take a mate, or *par'Mach'kai*, from amongst their comrades. Klingon commanders do not consider this to cause any conflicts of interests since a Klingon's sense of duty and honor should overcome any personal attachments they might have.

In their more serious moments, some—though by no means all—Klingons devote themselves to meditation and prayer, hoping to be granted visions of their semi-mythical leader, Kahless the Unforgettable. Like many Klingon ceremonies this involves the burning of candles and small furnaces, making parts of the ship even hotter and smokier than normal.

However, above all a Bird-of-Prey is a place of work, with every warrior and servant devoted to the service of the ship, and their captain.

The bridge is the operational nerve center of a Klingon Bird-of-Prey. It is located in the head section, in one of the most heavily armored and shielded sections of the ship, and therefore stands a small chance of surviving a catastrophic failure of the warp engines at the rear of the ship.

Its position on Deck 5 means that it is on the direct centerline of the ship, and the corridor that leads to it runs the entire length of the ship allowing personnel direct access to the engine rooms in the rear section of the ship's hull.

It is tied in to all the major ship's systems with a large data trunk running to the main computer core in the two decks below.

The command stations on the bridge can be configured to serve a variety of functions. This serves two purposes: first it allows commanders to configure the bridge in any manner they see fit (for example,

some captains prefer to have the tactical officer on the right, while others prefer to have him or her on the left); second, it allows stations to be reassigned if the ship is damaged in battle.

Each station employs touch-sensitive combined data and display panels that automatically reconfigure themselves as data is input and conditions change. The design of Klingon interfaces has been refined over the years to improve the crew's response times. Priority is given to accessing the weapons and defensive systems. The crew are rigorously drilled on their use on a daily basis. During these drills the stations are locked into simulation mode, which is almost indistinguishable from normal flight operations.

The stations can also be locked into a diagnostic mode and when this happens their functions are transferred to one of the free-standing consoles in the center of the bridge.

▼ The bridge is located in the head of the ship and has direct access to all her critical systems.

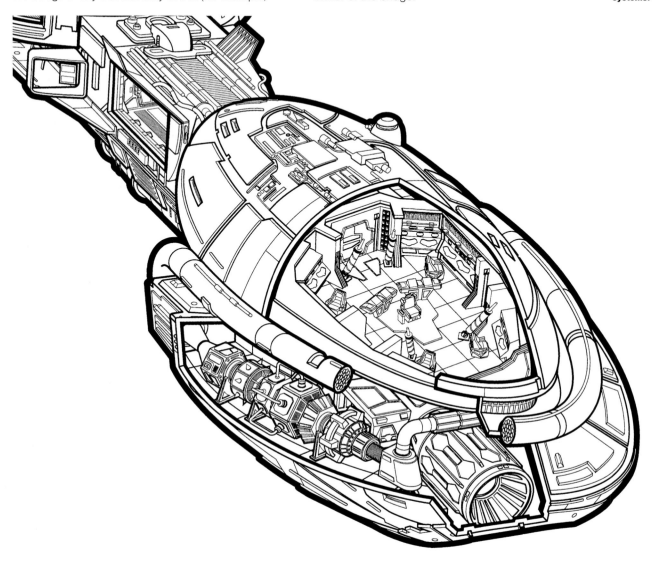

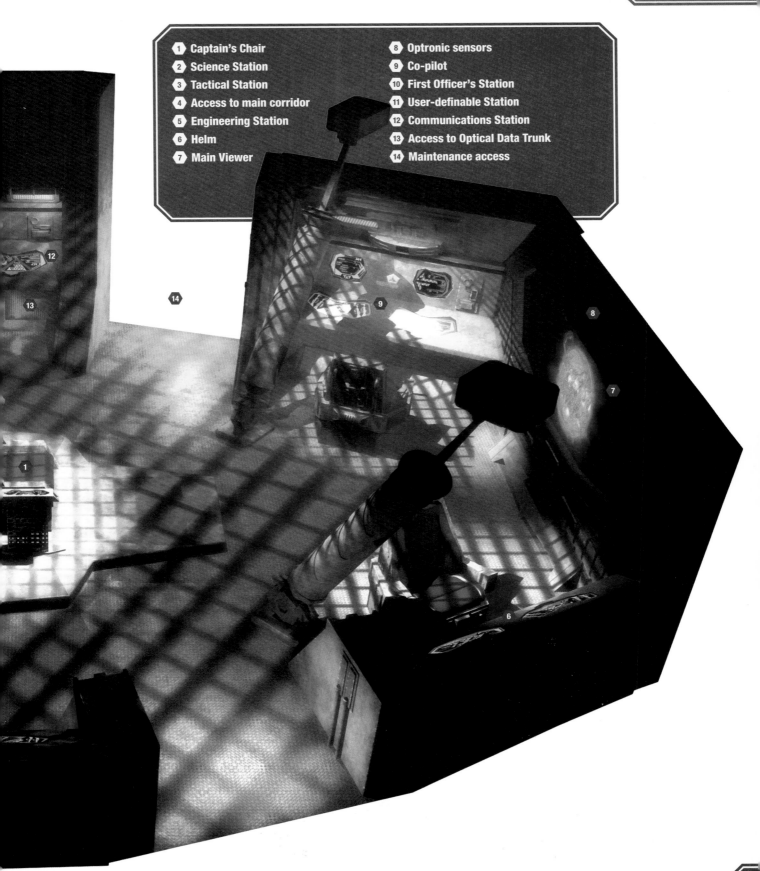

1. Captain's Chair
2. Science Station
3. Tactical Station
4. Access to main corridor
5. Engineering Station
6. Helm
7. Main Viewer
8. Optronic sensors
9. Co-pilot
10. First Officer's Station
11. User-definable Station
12. Communications Station
13. Access to Optical Data Trunk
14. Maintenance access

CAPTAIN'S CHAIR
Hod quS

The captain's chair is located in the middle of the room placing the captain in the center of the action. It has very few controls, but a small panel built into the armrest allows the captain to access the communications system. In emergencies he can fire the disruptors and torpedoes, but this depends on targeting information being displayed on the main viewer or simply firing blind based on visual input from the viewer. This small console also allows the captain to activate the ship's autodestruct system.

MAIN VIEWER
jIH'a'

At the front of the bridge is the main viewer— a large display panel that is used to provide a variety of data to the bridge crew. Under normal operating conditions it is configured to show the heading immediately in front of the ship, almost as if it were a window, but it can draw on the sensors to provide a view of any angle around the ship at a variety of magnifications. During combat, the tactical officer can transfer his readouts to the viewer, providing a data overlay that records the condition of any enemy vessels, and shows input from the targeting scanners.

When a communication channel is opened, the main computer automatically switches the main viewer to show the incoming signal. Optronic scanners above the viewer record the images and audio that are then transmitted back to the other party.

HELM
Degh

The two stations at the front of the bridge are almost always configured as helm and navigation. They are tied into one another, with all the functions of one station duplicated on the other. In normal operational mode, one station takes responsibility for piloting the ship and data from the immediate vicinity, while the other deals with long-range navigational data and monitoring the condition of the subspace field in cooperation with the engineering officer. During combat mode, they can be reconfigured to act as the pilot's and co-pilot's stations with one officer standing by to take control if the other is injured.

The helm is pre-programmed with a series of tactical maneuvers—divided into attack and defensive patterns—that have been agreed and practised with the commanding officer. These are determined individually on each ship, and are designed to the exact specifications of the particular Bird-of-Prey's

► The captain's chair is positioned in the middle of the bridge, making it absolutely clear that it is the seat of power.

◀ The main viewer is normally set to display immediately in front of the ship, but can display a wide range of information.

weapons and defenses. However, they are based on the standard maneuvers laid out in the famous 23rd century text, *The Book of Kang*.

Long-range headings are input by the navigation officer but are calculated by the navigational computer, which uses long-range sensors to determine the best possible route. At faster-than-light (FTL) velocities the course corrections are performed at such high speed that the helm and navigation officer can do little more than monitor the situation. He or she is provided with a constant stream of data about the condition of the ship, the actual velocities achieved, identified hazards on the course and the recommended actions needed to avoid them. At FTL speeds, the helm officer can input a new course but cannot take direct manual control of the ship.

At sublight speeds and in atmospheric operations the helm can take direct control of the ship's systems and fly the ship manually. He or she has access to the RCS (Reaction Control System) thrusters and the landing gear.

▼ The twin helm and navigation consoles are used to input and monitor the ship's heading

ENGINEERING STATION
jon yaH

The engineering station provides information about all the ship's systems, not just the engines. The station is directly tied into the engineering computer systems and allows for direct control of the warp and impulse engines, plasma flow and the warp wings. These functions are duplicated in the engineering section, but actually controlled from the bridge. An open communication channel is always maintained between the bridge and main engineering.

The displays at this station provide a constant update on the condition of the ship's systems, and during battle this is the primary station used for damage control. The engineering officer also has direct control of the emergency bulkheads used to seal off any badly damaged or uninhabitable areas of the ship.

The engineering officer works in close concert with both the helm and science officers.

SCIENCE STATION
QeD yaH

The science station provides a constant stream of information from the ship's sensors, with a particular emphasis on the condition of any nearby vessels,

which Klingons always consider to pose a threat. During battle, the science officer has primary responsibility for monitoring the condition of enemy vessels, including the nature of an enemy's weapons and the condition of their engines. The science officer provides recommendations to the captain and tactical officer. This data is automatically shared with the tactical station, but is accessed at a lower menu level. The dedicated computers also provide analysis of stellar phenomena that may pose a threat to the ship, for the control of long- and short-range probes and the ship's transporter systems.

TACTICAL STATION
wly yaH

The primary purpose of the tactical station is to control the ship's weapons and shields. The station displays show the condition of the ship's disruptors, indicating the exact power levels that are available, and status of the photon torpedo launcher and bays. Typically, on Klingon ships the weapons officer takes direct manual control of the weapons and fires them 'by eye' rather than relying on computer-guided systems. However, the station has a direct connection to the helm station, which provides telemetry showing the weapons

▶ **The science and tactical stations are normally positioned on the captain's left.**

officer where the ship is in any given maneuver and recommending when the weapons should be activated. The tactical officer is also responsible for making recommendations to the captain but the strict hierarchy on a Bird-of-Prey means that he or she is normally the 'trigger man' carrying out the captain's or first officer's orders. In fact, during combat weapons control is often transferred to the free-standing consoles behind the captain, which are operated by the first officer.

FIRST OFFICER STATION
yaS wa'DIch yaH

The first officer typically operates two free-standing consoles behind the captain's chair. These consoles don't have a dedicated function but are designed to take direct control of any, and all, the other bridge consoles. During normal flight operations, the first officer monitors the condition of all the other stations, ensuring that the ship is running smoothly and the other officers are performing their duties. During combat, the first officer often takes direct control of either the helm or the weapons stations. The consoles have a dedicated connection to the main computer and provide a backup if any of the stations are damaged.

BULKHEADS
tlhoy'mey

The bulkheads around the bridge contain dedicated computer subprocessors, which provide immediate calculating power for the bridge stations.

Optical data trunks connect the individual stations to the sensor arrays, with a wide-branching data trunk connecting the stations to one another, allowing data to be pooled and transferred between the stations. In addition a secondary data trunk connects all the stations to the main computer.

▲ The engineering console, to the captain's right, has direct control of all the ship's systems.

▼ The first officer mans a series of consoles that can take control of any of the ship's functions.

The standard Bird-of-Prey has a crew of 36, of whom eight are officers. The remaining crew consists of between 24 and 26 warriors and between two and four servants. It is common for women to serve on ships, though they normally only make up a small percentage of the crew.

The officers are the most senior members of the crew, and each of them is responsible for a department, which always consists of two warriors who act as deputies to the officer, performing the department's duties when the officer is off duty. The departments are: command, weapons, helm and navigation, engineering and science.

CAPTAIN
HoD

There are four command officers starting with the captain, who is supported by a first, a second and a third officer. His responsibility is to command the ship, making all the important tactical decisions. The crew consider their lives to be in his hands and a good captain takes the responsibility seriously. He expects total obedience from his crew and in return they expect him to lead them to glorious victories and to bring honor to the ship and the crew.

The captain has the right to promote officers, and even to elevate a servant to warrior status. He has to be careful how he uses this power since any unjustified promotions or signs of favoritism are likely to result in a challenge.

FIRST OFFICER
yaS wa'DIch

According to Klingon tradition the first officer 'serves the captain but stands for the crew'. When the first officer takes over command of the crew, they surrender their battle record to him, which should provide a healthy list of victories. He then pledges the crew's lives in the service of the captain.

He is tasked with the day-to-day running of the ship, scheduling drills, assigning duties, and ensuring that the crew and the ship are functioning at peak efficiency. It is also his role to offer tactical advice to the captain, presenting different options in combat. In many ways he is seen as a captain in waiting and must be ready to assume command if the captain is incapacitated. He must also be strong enough to challenge the captain if he sees any signs of weakness or feels that the captain is leading the crew down a dishonorable path.

▶ **During the Dominion War, Martok famously took the disgraced Worf into his house and made him his first officer.**

SECOND OFFICER
yaS cha'DIch

The second officer is effectively an understudy for the first officer, and normally performs similar duties on one of the other shifts. Unlike the first officer, he has little direct contact with the captain, but may be closer to the crew. His recommendations are fed directly to the first officer. By tradition, he takes particular responsibility for the condition of engineering and weapons.

THIRD OFFICER
yaS wejDIch

The third officer is a junior position normally held by a young man, who is learning the needs of command. Thus the third officer serves at a variety of different posts around the ship, learning the skills of all the departments. Unlike the first and second officers, he is unlikely to take a shift in command of the ship during combat missions, but he will take shifts in command during peacetime.

HELMSMAN
DeghwI'

The helmsman is responsible for laying in a course and controlling the ship's speed. For faster-than-light travel the on-board computers provide recommendations about the best possible course, based on the position of stellar objects, but the helmsman is responsible for monitoring progress and for compensating for any unexpected activity. The Klingons place great store in a helmsman's ability to pilot a ship manually, and the helmsman must be capable of performing a wide variety of maneuvers both in open space and in a planetary atmosphere. He or she is also responsible for learning a wide variety of tactical maneuvers, which will be specifically laid out by the captain.

WEAPONS OFFICER
nuHpin

The weapons officer assigned to the bridge has direct control of all the ship's weaponry. Since this can vary from vessel to vessel, it is vital that he is completely familiar with all the systems and their capabilities. Weapons control is routed to the station on the bridge, but there is also a warrior manning the weapons room deep within the ship, with whom the weapons officer is in direct contact as well as monitoring the tactical computers.

The weapons officer has the duty of studying any and all enemy vessels the crew are likely to encounter,

◄◄ For a Klingon warrior surviving into old age is unfortunate. The great hero Kor managed to secure a junior post on the *Rotarran* that ultimately allowed him to earn a glorious death.

◄ It is common for Klingon women to serve on a Bird-of-Prey although they rarely rise to command.

and warp and impulse engines, transferring power between the different systems as necessary.

The remaining crew members are either warriors or servants. The surgeon is a warrior, but the six engineers and three cooks are all servants.

THE CREW
beq

The crew complement normally consists of 16 warriors, who provide cover for the senior staff on the bridge and man the weapons room. Warriors are not officers and did not attend the training academy on Ogat. Despite their lower status they are considered to be the backbone of the Klingon fleet, and every Klingon child aspires to become a warrior. They are trained in all the ship's systems and are often every bit as capable as their superiors. They spend a considerable amount of their time in one of the ship's main communal areas—the training hall.

The walls of this large open space are hung with bladed weapons such as *bat'leths* and *mek'leths*. This area is used for any occasions when the captain needs to assemble the crew, for example when accepting new crew members aboard or when briefing a boarding party, but above all it is used for weapons training and martial arts drills.

The center of the room is left open, essentially like a gym floor and it is common for all crew members to spend at least one hour a day here performing *Mok'bara* drills, with and without *bat'leths*, and sparring with one another. Full combat sparring is banned during active combat missions because of the risk of serious injury.

For Klingons injuries are a part of everyday life. They can be sustained during sparring, disagreements about status, even in mating. Accordingly, Klingons place great importance on medical treatment. Every Klingon learns basic field medicine from an early age and can perform stitches and set bones almost as soon as they can wield a *bat'leth*.

◤ The half-Klingon-half-human Alexander Rozhenko became something of a mascot for the *Rotarran*, making up in luck what he lacked in skill.

to ensure that he has as much knowledge as possible about their offensive capabilities and any weaknesses that the Klingons might be able to exploit.

SCIENCE OFFICER
QeDpln

It is a misconception that Klingons have no interest in science; it's simply that they are most interested in the kind of science that can be used in combat. The science officer is a vital member of the command crew and is responsible for interpreting all the sensor data that the ship collects. This is vital when dealing with unfamiliar stellar phenomena that could pose a threat to the ship or render the cloaking device ineffective. Before teleporting to a planet or landing on the surface, the science officer will assess the safety of the atmosphere and make recommendations about the best possible landing site.

In combat, he or she will advise on the condition of enemy vessels and collects as much data as possible on their performance, which is then shared with the weapons and engineering officers in order to devise effective tactics.

ENGINEERING OFFICER
jonpln

The engineering officer is a role distinct from that of engineer. He or she serves on the bridge and is responsible for monitoring the condition of the ship at all times. He or she also has control of the cloaking device. This role is roughly the equivalent of an Ops officer on a Federation starship. During combat, he or she is responsible for damage control and for monitoring the condition of the cloaking device, shields

DOCTOR/SURGEON
Haqwl'

Every Bird-of-Prey's crew includes a doctor or surgeon—the Klingon word *Haqwl'* literally translates as bone mender—who specializes in medical treatment. Although the surgeon is not an officer, it is still one of the most respected positions on board ship. There is no warrior worth his salt who has not been injured seriously enough to owe his or her life—or at least a limb—to the surgeon.

The medical bay is located on Deck 5, and consists

of three distinct areas: an emergency treatment room, which is dominated by an examination bench; a surgical and recovery ward, where more serious injuries are treated and the severely wounded have the chance to recover and the surgeon's quarters. By actually living in the medical bay, the surgeon is always available.

Even when the ship isn't in combat mode the surgeon is kept busy treating the kind of minor wounds, such as cuts and cracked ribs, that are the inevitable consequence of the Klingon way. During actual combat, whenever Alert Status One is called, one other warrior is assigned to the medical bay to perform triage.

Klingon medicine focuses on providing immediate treatment and getting a warrior back to his station as quickly as possible, often with the aid of stimulants. Wherever possible treatment is provided on the examination bench. The surgeon typically injects a combined stimulant and pain killer, before using a *petqaD* to bond broken bones in place and a dermal regenerator to suture any wounds. Typical turnaround times allow an injured crewman to return to his post within seven minutes.

In more serious cases, where there is severe

internal bleeding or a limb or an eye is in serious danger of being lost, the surgeon restricts the injured warrior to the medical bay. The typical medical bay has two recovery beds and one surgical bay. In cases of life-threatening injuries, the patient may be placed in stasis.

If the surgeon deems that an injury will seriously impede a warrior's life whatever the treatment, the warrior is simply allowed to die. For example, Klingons

▲ Klingon warriors hope for nothing more than a glorious death in battle and hope to die while serving on a Bird-of-Prey.

◀ Brawling is a part of life on a Klingon ship and is used to establish and maintain a hierarchy amongst the crew.

have never developed sophisticated treatments for paralysis caused by neurological damage.

ENGINEERS
jonwI'

The six engineers are based in Main Engineering, where the warp engines require almost constant supervision. There are always two on duty—in order to provide cover if one of them should be killed in action. An engineer is a specialist and, since he or she is not a warrior, has a lesser status than any of the bridge crew. In fact, the engineers are under the direct command of the Engineering Officer on the bridge. The Klingon attitude is that the engineer is basically a mechanic, who is responsible for keeping the ship running at peak efficiency, but nowhere near as important as the pilot or the command officers who set priorities.

All Klingons are trained to have more than a passing familiarity with the ship's engine systems, and no less a person than the Klingon hero and Dahar Master Kor boasted that he once personally stripped down his ship's cloaking device. However, Klingon warriors have little time for monitoring the exact intermix formulas and plasma pressures in their engines, which they consider to be a menial task.

The engineers' duty is to the ship above all else, and their lives are literally not worth living if important ship's systems fail during a mission.

COOK
vutwI'

The cook is possibly the next most important person on the ship, even though they have the lowest possible status. Unlike other spacefaring races the Klingons do not eat, or approve of, replicated or even cooked food, which they consider to be artificial and burnt. A proper Klingon meal consists of freshly slaughtered or live food. The cook doesn't actually cook anything—instead he is an expert butcher, who knows how to season food, often with extremely powerful spices.

The mess hall itself is the social center of the ship, and off-duty crew members will invariably congregate here. The mess hall is dominated by a huge table at which each crew member has a designated place. Seating is strictly hierarchical, with the most honored positions being at the heads and in the center. New crew members have to fight for their place at table and it is common for crewmen to brawl in this area. This is perfectly normal and is not seen as a problem.

▶ **The mess hall is the social center of a Bird-of-Prey and used by every member from the lowest servant to the captain.**

◄◄ Klingons like their food freshly butchered and routinely carry a stock of live targs.

◄ The state of a ship can often be judged by the quality of its *gagh*. If things are good, the *gagh* will be live and active, perfect for eating.

The entire crew uses the mess hall, including the captain. There are no private dining halls on a Klingon vessel and a good commander is seen eating, drinking and laughing with his crew. When he is exceptionally busy, a commanding officer may choose to eat in his quarters but he would be unwise to do so on a regular basis. The cooks work hard to keep the mess hall supplied with food and drink. Kahless himself once said that a general's first victory is keeping his army well fed. A bad cook on Bird-of-Prey is unheard of, not least because Klingons use violence to express their dissatisfaction with poorly prepared food.

The three cooks—one is always on duty—operate out of a galley that is adjacent to the Mess Hall, which consists of a large preparation area, pens for livestock, which include live targs, and vats of foodstuffs such as *gagh*—live serpent worms that are one of the staples of the Klingon diet.

Only the cook himself has access to the ship's supply of bloodwine, which is always kept under lock and key and dispensed only as the captain sees fit. Other senior officers are permitted to bring their own bloodwine on board but this is also distributed at the captain's pleasure.

Accommodation on board a Bird-of-Prey is famously austere, even though there is more than enough room to provide spacious quarters for every one of the 36 crew members. The senior officers—the captain, first and second officers—normally have their own private quarters that include an office space where they can prepare for the day, communicate with the Klingon High Command and hold audiences with junior crew members. Other crew members often share their quarters and have little room for

private possessions. Typically beds are little more than alcoves built into the bulkheads and crewmen have a simple locker in which to store their trophies and personal effects.

To the Klingon mind, life aboard ship is about one thing—the glory of battle and everything else is secondary. Like the ideal Klingon warrior, the crew is disciplined and of one mind, and their ship is stripped back and lean.

▼ A happy Klingon ship often rings out to the sound of opera as the crew sing at their work.

Life on board is divided into three six-hour shifts, with at least 12 crew members always on duty. Although the captain is formally part of the shift system he tends to stand outside it and will be on the bridge whenever he feels his presence is necessary. Typically, the captain and first officer will work the same shift, though in theory they each command a separate shift.

The three rosters—or *ghom ngoy'* in Klingon—operate in a strict hierarchy, with the most senior roster including all the command officers except the second officer, who typically heads up the second roster, and the third officer who moves between shifts. Whenever the ship is entering combat, the shift system is abandoned and all the senior crew members take their stations. The first roster takes command with all the other warriors on standby to replace anyone who falls in battle.

FIRST SHIFT [DUTY SHIFT]
Qu' poH wa'DIch

Officers and warriors on the duty shift are responsible for operating the ship. The bridge should always be staffed with at least four crew members, with two warriors assigned to the engineering section, one to the sensors, one to the weapons room and one to the medical bay, and one servant to the galley.

Klingon crews are rigorously drilled. Each duty shift involves a session of battle drills with the computers programmed to simulate the sensor inputs that would be generated in an actual battle. The drills take place under the supervision of the first or second officers and take two different forms. The first of these is used when the crew is on active battle duty. The computers are put into a simulation mode. Weapons are not fired and the ship continues on its pre-programmed course, but the consoles all behave as if the ship really were at combat and to the untrained eye it is impossible to distinguish the data they provide from the real thing.

This form of drill is necessary when the ship is cloaked or in times of war when it is important to conserve photon torpedoes. However the Klingons are keenly aware of the limitations of this kind of training and wherever possible they prefer to train with live weapons and active helm control. In these kinds of drills the computer still generates an artificial attacker, but the ship responds to the crew's commands, weapons are fired, the cloak is engaged

and dropped and the ship actually performs the maneuvers ordered by the helmsman.

Many Klingon captains regard this kind of drill as insufficiently realistic and it is quite common for them to drop out of warp and spend time shooting asteroids as target practice.

The drills are supervised by the first or second officer, who note reaction times and administer discipline to crew members who do not meet the standard expected of them.

The officers assigned to the weapons room start each shift by recalibrating and testing the targeting sensors, and once every third shift stripping down and rebuilding the ship's supply of disruptor rifles.

SECOND SHIFT [LEISURE SHIFT]
Qu' poH cha'DIch

During the second shift the crew are at what loosely translates as leisure. In practice this means that they congregate in one of the two communal areas on the ship: the mess hall or the training hall. Off-duty crew members will invariably head to the mess hall rather than their extremely basic quarters and at least some crew members can always be found here. Meals are served at the beginning of each shift and it is common for the entire shift to eat together.

Even outside of 'formal' meal times the mess hall is furnished with a constant supply of *gagh* and dishes such as *bregit* lung. Other delicacies such as heart of *targ* or *pipius* claw are reserved for special occasions such as a significant victory.

On a successful ship, the captain will ensure there is a plentiful supply of bloodwine, but during active combat missions this is only consumed by the men on the second shift, ensuring the crew have time to sober up before they return to their duty stations.

During this shift crew members are also expected to practice hand-to-hand combat in the training hall, and to spend time studying tactics and the exact specifications of enemy ships.

Senior members of the staff, such as the first officer, consider this shift to be a working one and use it to perform their admin duties.

THIRD SHIFT [SLEEP SHIFT]
Qu' poH wejDIch

The third shift is reserved for sleep and most warriors will spend it in their quarters.

CREW SHIFT SYSTEM

CREW OF A BIRD-OF-PREY	FIRST SHIFT	SECOND SHIFT	THIRD SHIFT
CAPTAIN	DUTY: BRIDGE	OFFICE/LEISURE	SLEEP
FIRST OFFICER	OFFICE/LEISURE	DUTY: BRIDGE	SLEEP
SECOND OFFICER	OFFICE/LEISURE	SLEEP	DUTY: BRIDGE
THIRD OFFICER	DUTY: BRIDGE	OFFICE/LEISURE	SLEEP
COMMUNICATIONS OFFICER	DUTY: BRIDGE: COMMUNICATIONS	OFFICE/LEISURE	SLEEP
ENGINEERING OFFICER	DUTY: BRIDGE: ENGINEERING	OFFICE/LEISURE	SLEEP
HELMSMAN	DUTY: BRIDGE: HELM	OFFICE/LEISURE	SLEEP
SCIENCE OFFICER	DUTY: BRIDGE: SCIENCE	OFFICE/LEISURE	SLEEP
WEAPONS OFFICER	DUTY: BRIDGE: WEAPONS	OFFICE/LEISURE	SLEEP
ENGINEER	DUTY: ENGINEERING	OFFICE/LEISURE	SLEEP
ENGINEER	DUTY: ENGINEERING	OFFICE/LEISURE	SLEEP
COOK	DUTY: MESS HALL	OFFICE/LEISURE	SLEEP
DOCTOR/SURGEON	DUTY: SURGERY	OFFICE/LEISURE	SLEEP
WARRIOR	DUTY: WEAPONS ROOM	OFFICE/LEISURE	SLEEP
WARRIOR	SLEEP	DUTY: BRIDGE: COMMUNICATIONS	OFFICE/LEISURE
WARRIOR	SLEEP	DUTY: BRIDGE: ENGINEERING	OFFICE/LEISURE
WARRIOR	SLEEP	DUTY: BRIDGE: HELM	OFFICE/LEISURE
WARRIOR	SLEEP	DUTY: BRIDGE: SCIENCE	OFFICE/LEISURE
WARRIOR	SLEEP	DUTY: BRIDGE: WEAPONS	OFFICE/LEISURE
ENGINEER	SLEEP	DUTY: ENGINEERING	OFFICE/LEISURE
ENGINEER	SLEEP	DUTY: ENGINEERING	OFFICE/LEISURE
JUNIOR COOK	SLEEP	DUTY: MESS HALL	OFFICE/LEISURE
WARRIOR	SLEEP	DUTY: SURGERY	OFFICE/LEISURE
WARRIOR	SLEEP	DUTY: WEAPONS ROOM	OFFICE/LEISURE
WARRIOR	OFFICE/LEISURE	SLEEP	DUTY: BRIDGE: COMMUNICATIONS
WARRIOR	OFFICE/LEISURE	SLEEP	DUTY: BRIDGE: ENGINEERING
WARRIOR	OFFICE/LEISURE	SLEEP	DUTY: BRIDGE: HELM
WARRIOR	OFFICE/LEISURE	SLEEP	DUTY: BRIDGE: SCIENCE
WARRIOR	OFFICE/LEISURE	SLEEP	DUTY: BRIDGE: WEAPONS
ENGINEER	OFFICE/LEISURE	SLEEP	DUTY: ENGINEERING
ENGINEER	OFFICE/LEISURE	SLEEP	DUTY: ENGINEERING
ASSISTANT COOK	OFFICE/LEISURE	SLEEP	DUTY: MESS HALL
WARRIOR	OFFICE/LEISURE	SLEEP	DUTY: SURGERY
WARRIOR	OFFICE/LEISURE	SLEEP	DUTY: WEAPONS ROOM
WARRIOR	OFFICE/LEISURE	SLEEP	DUTY: WEAPONS ROOM

RAPTOR-CLASS

22ND C. BIRD-OF-PREY

D5-CLASS

B'REL-CLASS

K'TINGA-CLASS

VOR'CHA-CLASS

NEGH'VAR-CLASS

The Klingon fleet has always consisted of two basic types of vessel—small raiding and scouting ships such as the Bird-of-Prey and large capital ships such as the *K'Tinga*-class battlecruiser or the more recent *Vor'cha*-class attack cruiser. The first of these types of ship has often had a remit to stray far outside Klingon space, mounting raids on enemy colonies or carrying out intelligence missions. The Bird-of-Prey has been at the heart of this kind of activity since the Klingon Empire first achieved interstellar flight, and the 22nd-century (and even earlier) versions of the ship are instantly recognisable as being broadly similar to those in service today.

The larger capital ships from the *K'Tinga*-class battlecruiser to the vast *Negh'var* are normally tasked with patrolling the borders of Klingon space and maintaining order within the Empire, quelling rebellions and presenting a show of power. In times of war, they are used in mass assaults and planetary invasions.

It is not uncommon for a Klingon starship to remain in service for more than a century, since the Klingon Defense Force has always prioritized making the maximum number of ships available, rather than concentrating on fielding the most advanced fleet possible. The feudal nature of Klingon society also means that the Great Houses are reluctant to put a weapon away even when they have added a new and superior one. As the Klingon bards would have it, "There is no reason not to carry a sword and an axe."

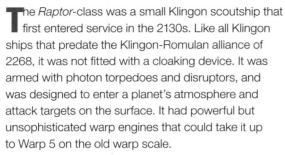

RAPTOR-CLASS

The *Raptor*-class was a small Klingon scoutship that first entered service in the 2130s. Like all Klingon ships that predate the Klingon-Romulan alliance of 2268, it was not fitted with a cloaking device. It was armed with photon torpedoes and disruptors, and was designed to enter a planet's atmosphere and attack targets on the surface. It had powerful but unsophisticated warp engines that could take it up to Warp 5 on the old warp scale.

The *Raptor*'s small size made it ideal for reconnaissance missions, but it was principally used in raiding missions along the borders of Klingon space, with the crew mounting brief and deadly assaults on the enemies of the Empire in a bid to prevent their expansion and to gather intelligence that could be fed back to

the Klingon Defense Force prior to a more sustained assault or invasion. Like all vessels of the period it was designed to operate for extended periods of up to six months away from space stations or Klingon planets. The crew would routinely supplement their supplies by mounting raids on other species, meaning that in some cases *Raptors* operated away from Klingon space for up to a year. However, *Raptors* normally operated within relatively close range of the larger battle cruisers that led the expansion of the Empire during this period.

The *Raptor* was less heavily armed than this era's Bird-of-Prey, which was in service at the same time and had a similar mission profile, and, unlike the Bird-of-Prey, it used conventional warp nacelles rather than warp wings.

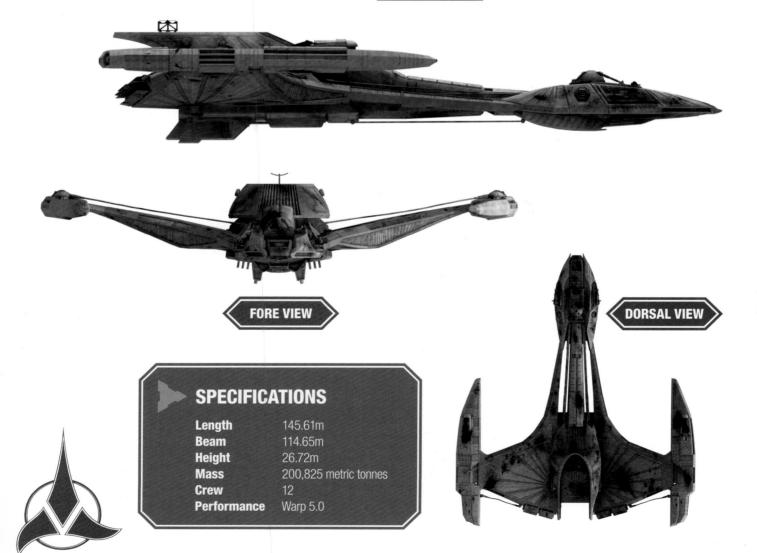

STARBOARD VIEW

FORE VIEW

DORSAL VIEW

SPECIFICATIONS

Length	145.61m
Beam	114.65m
Height	26.72m
Mass	200,825 metric tonnes
Crew	12
Performance	Warp 5.0

The 22nd-century version of the Bird-of-Prey was a relatively small raiding and scouting vessel with a crew of 48. It had a top speed of warp 6, making it easily capable of interstellar travel. It was the most heavily armed Klingon vessel of the era with eight separate disruptor banks, including twin disruptor cannons that were mounted on the underside and could fire in a 360-degree radius, and a forward-mounted disruptor that fired from a position next to the forward photon torpedo launcher in the familiar position in the nose. A second photon torpedo launcher fired aft.

Unlike the similar *Raptor*-class it used energised warp wings, which are the signature design feature of this class of ship.

Despite its relatively small size it carried a shuttlecraft, which could be launched from the rear of the ship in a bay below the impulse engines. Tactically, the Bird-of-Prey had two significant weaknesses—a lack of aft weaponry and armament and an exposed plasma junction that was vulnerable to attack if an enemy knew the exact spot to target.

In this era the Bird-of-Prey was one of the most far-ranging ships in the Klingon fleet and their captains were at liberty to fly far beyond the limits of Klingon space. In fact, Birds-of-Prey were seen as far away as Earth. They operated without support from larger, capital ships, meaning their crews had extraordinary opportunities to earn honour.

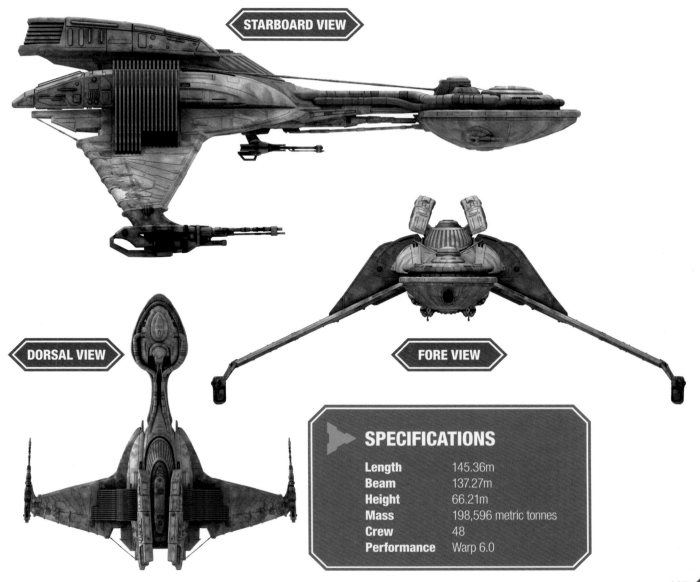

STARBOARD VIEW

DORSAL VIEW

FORE VIEW

SPECIFICATIONS

Length	145.36m
Beam	137.27m
Height	66.21m
Mass	198,596 metric tonnes
Crew	48
Performance	Warp 6.0

The D5 battle cruiser first entered service in the 2120s and remained an essential part of the Klingon Defense Force well into the 23rd century, when the last remaining ships in service were fitted with some of the first cloaking devices. One of the most famous D5 battle cruisers—the *Klothos*—was Kor's ship when he led the attack on Caleb IV.

When they were first introduced, the D5s made up the backbone of the Klingon Defense Force and routinely patrolled Klingon space, defending it against all enemies. They were also in the vanguard of any planetary assault and had the firepower to devastate a planet from orbit. In its time, it was the most powerful ship in the fleet and no less a person than Admiral Krell adopted one as his flagship.

They were heavily armed with multiple disruptor cannons and photon torpedoes. Like other Klingon ships of the period, it was fitted with a double disruptor cannon that was mounted below the ship and could fire in a 360-degree radius. It also had state-of-the-art sensors that were the equal of anything in the Starfleet or Vulcan fleets.

The D5's spaceframe could be adapted for use as a freighter when it was stripped of its major weaponry. Unlike the Bird-of-Prey it used conventional warp nacelles rather than energised warp wings. Although they were slightly larger than scouting ships such as the *Raptor* and Bird-of-Prey they could achieve higher speeds and could sustain Warp 6 for extended periods of time. However, they rarely operated outside of Klingon space unless they were part of an invasion force.

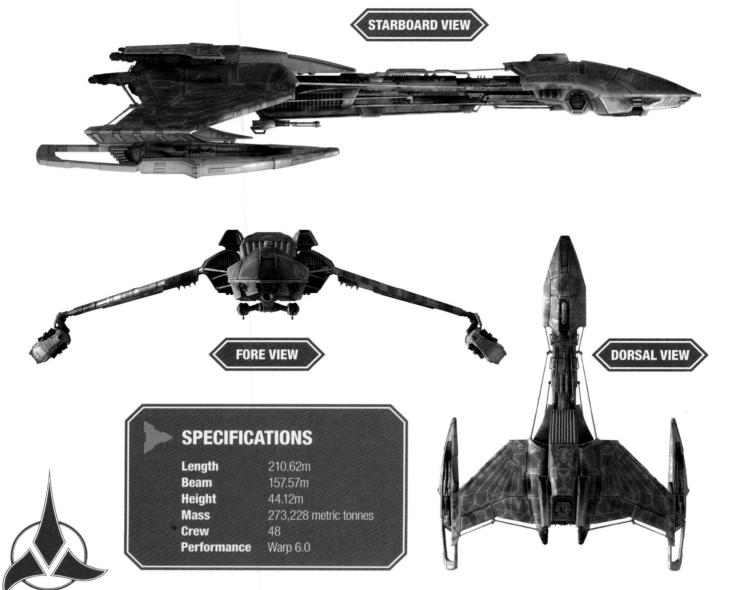

STARBOARD VIEW

FORE VIEW

DORSAL VIEW

SPECIFICATIONS

Length	210.62m
Beam	157.57m
Height	44.12m
Mass	273,228 metric tonnes
Crew	48
Performance	Warp 6.0

The *K'Tinga*-class battle cruiser formed the backbone of the Klingon fleet that patrolled the borders of Federation space in the mid to late 23rd century. It was one of the longest serving ship designs in the Klingon Defense Force and is very closely related to the *D5*- and *D7*-class battlecruisers, which followed the same basic layout, although the surface details were quite different. While not a true *K'Tinga*-class, which refers to the exact internal equipment, a predecessor of this class was in service as early as 2151.

Ships of this class were roughly analogous to the Federation's *Constitution*-class ships, which were their counterparts in the abortive Federation-Klingon war of 2267. In the 2290s the *K'Tinga* was the most advanced type of ship in the Klingon fleet and one of them served as Chancellor Gorkon's flagship, *Kronos One*, until his assassination by General Chang.

In the 2270s the *K'Tinga*-class was among the first Klingon ships to be fitted with a cloaking device. The standard layout for a ship of this era featured disruptors and photon torpedoes, with some ships of this type using an experimental concussive charge.

Far more advanced ships using the same basic spaceframe remained in service in the later 24th century and played a significant role in the Dominion War alongside the more advanced *Vor'cha*-class ships that were intended to replace them. Some of these ships used a forward mounted disruptor bank that could be fired from the navigational deflector around the photon torpedo launcher.

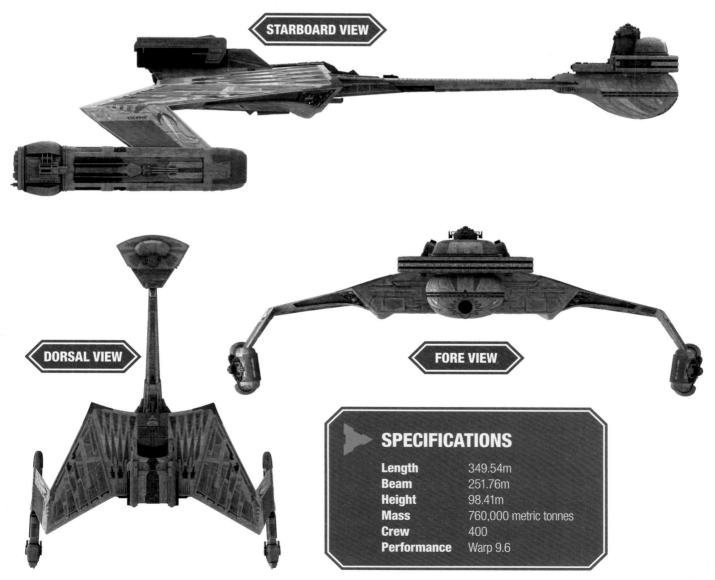

STARBOARD VIEW

DORSAL VIEW

FORE VIEW

SPECIFICATIONS

Length	349.54m
Beam	251.76m
Height	98.41m
Mass	760,000 metric tonnes
Crew	400
Performance	Warp 9.6

When the *Vor'cha*-class attack cruiser entered service in 2365 it was the most advanced and largest ship in the Klingon fleet. Ships of this class were intended as a direct replacement for the ageing *K'Tinga*-class and followed the same basic layout, but the technology was completely rethought from a 23rd-century perspective. The decision to develop ships of this nature was taken by K'mpec himself, who hoped this new class of ship would reinforce his own position within the Empire and provide a realistic counterpart to large Federation and Romulan vessels such as the *Galaxy*- and *D'deridex*-classes. As such the *Vor'cha* was also far larger than the *K'Tinga*-class and could effectively be a small mobile town—for example when serving as the flagship—or a troop transport.

Before this, the Klingon shipyards had attempted to produce the same results by scaling up the Bird-of-Prey to vast sizes.

Initially, very few *Vor'cha*-class ships were available and they were controlled only by high-ranking officials and the leaders of the Great Houses. The prototype, the *I.K.S. Vor'cha* became K'mpec's flagship until he was poisoned by fellow High Council member Duras. However, the design rapidly gained favour and soon formed a significant part of the Klingon Defense Force. They were made from standard Klingon components and could be easily mass produced. As a result they played a major role in the Dominion War.

STARBOARD VIEW

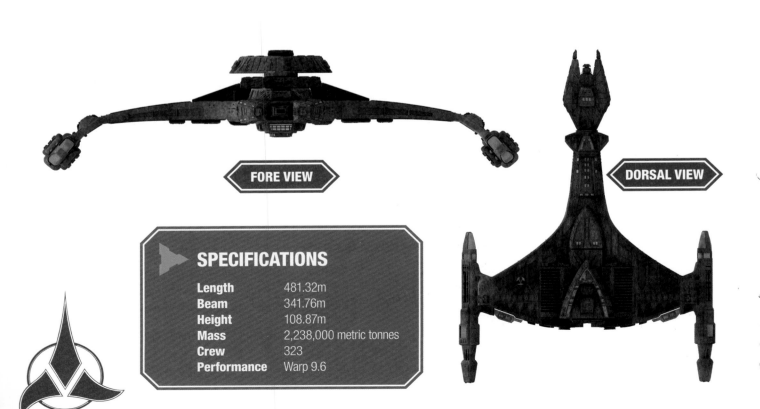

FORE VIEW

DORSAL VIEW

SPECIFICATIONS

Length	481.32m
Beam	341.76m
Height	108.87m
Mass	2,238,000 metric tonnes
Crew	323
Performance	Warp 9.6

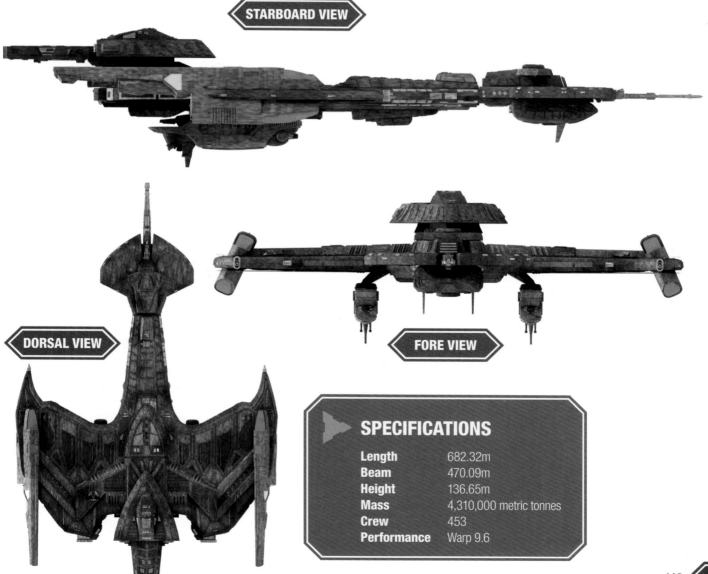

When Gowron became High Chancellor of the Klingon Empire he immediately commissioned a new and upgraded version of the attack cruiser that would serve as his flagship. The result was the *I.K.S. Negh'var*, a heavily armed vessel that is still the largest ship ever to serve in the Klingon Defense Force. Fitted with 20 disruptors and four torpedo launchers, she was a flying arsenal and was able to carry more than 2,500 troops.

To date the *Negh'var* is the only ship of its class and it is widely regarded as an anomaly that was created to show Gowron's prestige rather than for legitimate military reasons. The *Negh'var* was rushed into service and employed many experimental technologies that were considered impractical for mass production, and had such a high energy output that it required significant re-engineering of the cloaking system that pushed its power requirements to the absolute limit.

Most Klingon commanders believe that in strictly military terms the resources needed to produce ships of this class would be better devoted to producing a larger number of smaller ships. Nevertheless, the *Negh'var* was an impressive sight that inspired fear in almost any species that encountered her. She served as Gowron's flagship during the Dominion War, and led the Klingon invasion of Cardassian space in 2372. However, when Martok assumed power he had little time for the *Negh'var,* preferring to keep his flag aboard the *B'rel*-class *I.K.S. Rotarran*.

STARBOARD VIEW

DORSAL VIEW

FORE VIEW

SPECIFICATIONS

Length	682.32m
Beam	470.09m
Height	136.65m
Mass	4,310,000 metric tonnes
Crew	453
Performance	Warp 9.6

ENGLISH	KLINGON	pIqaD
accelerate	chung	
access	naw'	
accommodate	ma'	
activate	chu'	
advance	Duv	
aft	'o'	
airlock	HIchDal	
alarm	ghum	
alert	ghuHmoH	
altitude	'Iv	
ammunition	nIch	
analysis	poj	
antimatter	rugh	
appear	nargh	
approach	ghoS	
ascend	Sal	
asteroid	ghopDap	
atmosphere	muD	
attack	HIv	
attitude-control thrusters	lolSeHcha	
back (away from)	DoH	
battle	may'	
beam (transporter)	jol	
beside	retlh	
between	joj	
big	tIn	
blame	pIch	
block (prevent)	bot	
board (go aboard)	tlj	
boundary	veH	
brave	yoH	
break (rules)	bIv	
bridge (of ship)	meH	
build up (take form)	chen	
captain	HoD	
careful	yep	
careless	yepHa'	
cargo	tep	
catastrophe	lot	
cease (stop)	mev	
center	botlh	
chair	quS	
change	choH	

ENGLISH	KLINGON	pIqaD
charge (up)	Huj	
chase	tlha'	
chore (task)	Qu'	
chronometer	tlhaq	
circle	gho	
classification	buv	
climb	toS	
cloak (hide)	So'	
cloaking device	So'wI'	
close in	chol	
close (shut)	SoQmoH	
cloud	'eng	
cold	bIr	
collapse	Dej	
collide	paw'	
command	ra'	
communications officer	QumpIn	
computer	De'wI'	
contain (have inside)	ngaS	
control panel	SeHlaw	
cook	vut	
coordinates	Quv	
course (route)	He	
crew	beq	
cruise	qugh	
damage	QIH	
danger	Qob	
data	De'	
defeat	jey	
defective	Duy'	
defense	Hub	
deflectors	begh	
descend	ghIr	
destroy	Qaw'	
device	jan	
dilithium	cha'puj	
distance (range)	chuq	
distress call	Sotlaw'	
dock	vergh	
doctor (physician)	Qel	
door	lojmIt	
drill (military term)	qeq	
duel	Hay'	
duty	Qu'	
duty station	yaH	

Marc Okrand designed and developed the Klingon language and culture for the *STAR TREK* feature films and *STAR TREK: THE NEXT GENERATION*. He is the author of *The Klingon Dictionary*, published by Pocket Books, which was essential in the preparation of this table. The publisher also gratefully acknowledges Marc and members of the Klingon Language Institute for all the advice and assistance they have given during the preparation this Manual.

emergency	chach
empty	chIm
enemy	jagh
energize	rIH
energy (power)	HoS
engage (activate)	chu'
engine	jonta', QuQ
engineer	jonwI'
enter	'el
equipment	luch
evade	jun
exhaust	taQbang
explode	jor
fast	nom
fire (a weapon)	baH
fix (repair)	tI'
fleet (of ships)	yo'
flood	SoD
follow (a course)	ghoS
force field	Surchem
fuel	nIn
function (work)	Qap
galaxy	qIb
gas	SIp
gunner	baHwI'
helm	Degh
help (aid)	QaH
hot	tuj
hull	Som
identify	ngu'
impact (strike)	mup
impulse power	Hong
judge (estimate)	noH
kellicam	quell'qam
left (side)	poS
life-support system	yIntagh
loosen	QeyHa'moH
maintenance	leH
maneuver (direction)	QoD
manual (by hand)	ruQ
many (numerous)	law'
meteor	chunDab
mix	DuD
module	bobcho'
mutiny	qIQ

navigate	chIj
officer	yaS, 'utlh
outside	Hur
override	ngep
parallel	Don
phaser banks	pu'DaH
prepared (be prepared)	ghuS
project (on a screen)	HotIh
propel	vo'
ready (standing by)	SuH, Su'
right (side)	nIH
right (correct)	lugh
sabotage	Sorgh
satellite	SIbDoH
scanner	HotIhwI'
science officer	QeDpIn
section	'ay'
sector (zone)	mIch
security	Hung
sensor	noch
shield	yoD
ship (vessel)	Duj
sight (gunsight)	puS
slingshot	moy'bI'
smoke	tlhIch
space station	tengchaH
starship (starship class)	'ejDo'
sublight speed	gho'Do
system	pat
tactical display	wIy
technician	chamwI'
temperature	Hat
thrusters	chuyDaH
torpedo	peng
torpedo tube	chetvI', DuS
train (prepare)	qeq
transceiving device	HablI'
transport beam	jol
transport room	jolpa'
velocity	Do
visual display	HaSta
voyage	leng
warp drive	pIvghor
warp field	pIvchem
weapon	nuH

a		H		ng		S		y	4
b		I		o		St		'	5
ch		j		p		tlh		0	6
D		l		q		u		1	7
e		m		Q		v		2	8
gh		n		r		w		3	9

ACKNOWLEDGMENTS

The authors owe an enormous debt of gratitude to Gene Coon for inventing the Klingons in the first place and to John Colicos for his defining performance as Kor. In more recent years Burton Armus gave us our first real insight to life onboard a Bird-of-Prey and no one has contributed more to the exploration of Klingon culture than Ronald D. Moore. In many ways, it's fair to say that the modern Klingons are his invention.

When it comes to the Bird-of-Prey, we'd like to acknowledge the beautiful design work done by Nilo Rodis and Bill George who turned Leonard Nimoy's initial description into such a memorable spaceship.

In terms of this book enormous thanks are due to Rob Bonchune, who was unable to work on the project due to the sad loss of his mother, and Mike Okuda who provided an enormous cache of graphics. Jörg Hillebrand provided a nice set of research screencaps of the ship from various films and TV episodes, and Bernd Schneider maintains ex-astris-scientia.org as a terrific repository of *STAR TREK* knowledge and articles about sometimes thorny technical issues. Marian Cordry of CBS, Bill George of ILM and Kurt Kuhn of modelermagic.com all provided invaluable reference material and also deserve special thanks.